TRAPPED SECRETS

MALCOLM HOLLINGDRAKE

Book Thirteen in the Harrogate Crime Series

This novel is entirely a work of fiction. The names, characters and incidents portrayed in this novel are the work of the author's imagination. Any resemblance to actual persons (living or dead), events or localities is entirely coincidental.

ISBN 978-1-7393436-0-6

Also by Malcolm Hollingdrake

Bridging the Gulf

Shadows from the Past
Short Stories for Short Journeys

The Harrogate Crime Series

Only the Dead

Hell's Gate

Flesh Evidence

Game Point

Dying Art

Crossed Out

The Third Breath

Treble Clef

Threadbare

Fragments

Uncertainty of Reason

The Damascene Moment

The Merseyside Series – Published by Hobeck Books

Catch as Catch Can

Syn

Dedicated to

Debbie Hollingdrake

Thank you for your continued patience and understanding.

This book, number 13, is for you.

In loving memory of our dear friend

Gill Cleverdon

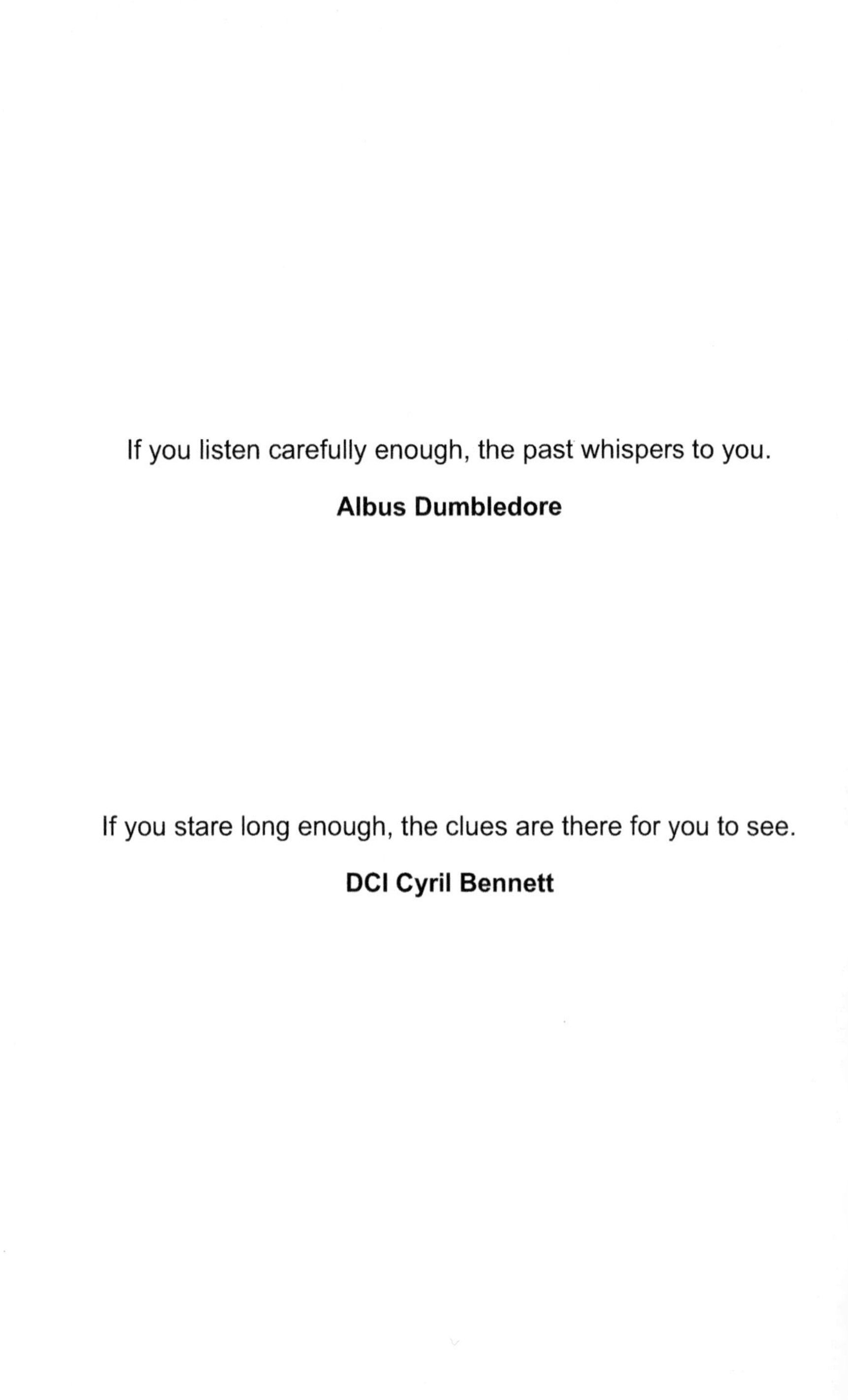

If you listen carefully enough, the past whispers to you.

Albus Dumbledore

If you stare long enough, the clues are there for you to see.

DCI Cyril Bennett

Chapter 1

The view through one of the many square panes that made up the large window set in the south wall of the library seemed clear when Cyril Bennett concentrated on the distant view. The sweeping garden, the topiaries set in two lines and the twin row of lime trees planted by royalty made Goldsborough Hall, set within parkland to the east of Knaresborough, famous. It was only when he stared at the glass itself, did he notice the unusual detail – it was not clear as we see glass today, but more a transparent, smoky grey holding myriad minute imperfections. But it was a specific area that attracted his focus and curiosity rather than the whole. An elongated bubble ran at a diagonal from the bottom left-hand corner of the pane, an area where the cream paint on the delicate wood frame had flaked as if it were an accomplice. The imperfection within the glass stopped near the centre. Cyril leaned closer as his hands danced around his dinner jacket to locate his glasses. "I need glasses to look at glass!" His words of frustration seemed to echo in the empty room yet quickly abated as he saw the funny side of the dilemma and a slight smile touched his lips.

The chimes from a clock he had passed somewhere along the corridor before entering the room seemed measured. It beat out the passing of time with muffled tones as if smothered by age itself. He slipped the glasses onto his nose and looked with a greater intensity. The deformity was real; an air bubble, trapped at the point of manufacture, was wafer thin. He stepped back allowing his finger to touch the area as he wondered what present day forensics might discover from the analysis of the air trapped within, air encapsulated maybe three hundred years ago. He thought immediately about the possibility that the bubble might contain a trapped whisper, a secret or an indiscretion – it was a romantic notion for him, but one that made his stomach tumble with a degree of excitement.

'You're turning into an old fool, Bennett.' The words had only just entered his head when he felt a hand rest on his shoulder. It made him jump.

"Sorry! I didn't mean to startle you. I knew you would either be in the bar or the library. You were miles away, Cyril."

Julie leaned her head against his shoulder as she admired the view of the garden. The line of trees was caught in the last rays of the setting sun, their leaves burnt with an amber richness that contrasted with the darkening sky.

"There's something about wood panelling, old tomes, leather Chesterfields and an open fire that attract coppers of a certain age. It runs in our DNA."

"You seemed very focused on something." Julie moved her head as if searching for the source of his attraction.

He laughed apologetically. "I was just looking at that."

He pointed to the imperfection. "It's like a ghost of the man that blew the glass, a captured breath of our ancestors, imprisoned for ever within that small, delicate bubble encapsulated within glass. A fossilised gasp." He turned, his glasses, perched on the end of his nose. "Just to think—" He did not finish his sentence.

"I'd hoped that *I* might capture *your* breath, Cyril. She stood back and turned three hundred and sixty degrees, her arms out to show the full flow of her gown.

Removing his glasses, his eyes ran up and down the body of the woman standing before him. He moved forward and kissed her forehead before stepping back and holding her hands out wide whilst admiring her appearance for the second time, either through guilt or pleasure. "Well doctor, you're certainly a sight for sore eyes and if I might be so bold as to ask, are you ready for the ball or should I say, Murder Mystery Night? However, be aware, your appearance this evening could certainly kill." His tone conspired to display a lack of enthusiasm for the event in which he was about to participate but his appreciation for her and the dress was evident.

"Thank you for agreeing to this. I know you —" She did not finish but took his hands and squeezed them gently before starting again. "I know you really are here under sufferance but please cheer up, nobody really dies! It's all fun and it's for charity." She adjusted his bow tie before angling her head as if to get a better view. "Perfect and as handsome as ever, Detective Chief Inspector!" Tugging his hand, she turned. "Come on, I need a drink before dinner and from the look on your face, Bennett, so do you with such a sour expression. You may suit a sweet sherry to begin the evening."

"Mmm! That's not very funny and if you keep on it will be a case of local senior detective discovered in the library with the sherry and a severe case of non-alcoholic poisoning."

She giggled and linked his elbow. "You and a sherry. Ha! Now that would be a sight for sore eyes!"

The popular annual charity event held at Goldsborough, now a hotel, seemed busier than she had anticipated, the noise increased the closer they came to the conservatory bar. A cocktail of music and voices seemed to meld, filling the ancient hall with contradictory excitement and energy. On entering, some heads turned and the sound from the live music immediately crystalised.

"It's Benny Goodman, Cyril." Julie's face demonstrated an immediate enthusiasm. "How very appropriate!"

"*Body and Soul*, I believe?" Cyril muttered as he took a deep breath. He smiled and nodded, not at the irony, but at the number of turned faces he recognised. A waiter approached. Cyril collected two flutes of what appeared to be Champagne but which he rightly guessed was actually Prosecco.

"DCI Bennett how lovely to see you!" Jonathan Cleverley moved directly in front of Cyril, a large man who gave the impression of a barge approaching a dock in a swell. "And Dr Julie, you look stunning! Thank you so much for coming. When I sent the invitation my wife said it wouldn't be your idea of a night out Cyril. Her words were – let me get this right – 'bringing coals to Newcastle' or was it 'a busman's holiday'? Either way, I think her intuition might have been correct, Detective Chief Inspector." He laughed loudly. “I expect you’ll find the killer immediately but if so, please give us mere mortals a sporting chance at discovering who done it!” He grinned at Julie and raised an eyebrow. “Unfortunately, Cyril, I’m not on your table this evening so I can’t crib any clues from you. Remember, we’re here for a good cause so nothing too serious.” He raised his glass. “Cheers!” With the same delicacy as his approach, he crashed his glass against that of Julie and then Cyril, the ringing being audible above the music. “As I say, welcome and do have fun.”

Chapter 2

The smear had arched across the van windscreen. The wiper blades had removed most of the mud but had left what seemed indelible, faint brown-grey lines that distorted the view. With a turn of the key and a flick of the wiper switch, water erupted onto the screen in two jets quickly followed by the swish of the blades until there was a squeal of protest and the glass was clear. Turning the key, again the hands moved instinctively back to the steering wheel.

To the left of the vehicle was a narrow strip of The Stray. It ran into a dip before rising again to meet Knaresborough Road. The scar of dark grey tarmac sliced the broader expansive section of sweeping grassland that was broken only by the occasional tree and pathways, if you disregarded the people of Harrogate enjoying the evening's fine weather. The lamps positioned some distance away, traditional in design, were lit, contradicting the clarity of the evening. The clear sky seemed to have slowed the coming dark, dusk was lingering longer than usual. Short wooden posts, soldier straight, were positioned along the grass edge to keep the cars from encroaching.

Eight fingers tapped the steering wheel with a regular,

gentle drumming beat, like that of a resting heart. To any observer it might have appeared to be a nervous twitch, a sign of growing impatience, but that would have been a clear error of judgement. Every movement was controlled and unhurried. It would take as long as it took. They would come, that was a given.

A jogger appeared from the left causing a head to turn, eyes to watch, as the runner crossed in front of the van. The semi-bent man demonstrated a struggling gait, there was evidence of a slight limp and the whole exercise looked uncomfortable. The runner's head did not turn but remained down, facing the route directly ahead until there was a brief glance to the right, a flick of the head to check the road was clear as he continued to cross. The fingers on the wheel never lost their cadence but maintained the same uninterrupted rhythm as if tapping out Morse code.

***

Contrary to his assumption, Cyril found the troupe of actors playing the various roles not only intriguing but also convincing. The evening's entertainment was set in the 1930s and the players were appropriately dressed adding to the hall's fitting ambience and mystery. The faux Inspector, amusingly named Clapper, was dressed in a business like fashion in a three piece suit. A watch chain and fob dangled from the pockets of the waistcoat and the culmination of style seemed to match the sharp trimmed moustache and Brilliantined hair. He stood before a seated female, a Miss Felicity Black, who was now quizzed before the audience about her whereabouts at the time of Colonel

Fitzgibbon's disappearance. Her black flapper dress sparkled as she moved in the candlelight. Cyril studied her whilst subconsciously suspending his disbelief. Julie watched in amazement as he scribbled notes of the proceedings on his napkin. The intensity of his concentration brought a warm smile of satisfaction to her lips. She sipped more wine and glanced at the burning candles in the centre of the table. The actor's voice, clear yet precise, and on occasion threatening, dominated the room.

"I've told you, Inspector, I saw him in the drawing room at about six. He had not yet dressed for dinner. He had been out with his dog." She inhaled on the black cigarette holder allowing a small cloud of smoke to drift from her lips as if it were an untruth. "The clock in the hallway chimed as he left the room. The dog remained by the fire."

Cyril turned to Julie and mouthed. "She knows more than she makes out does our Miss Black. You mark my words. She's not a smoker either."

Julie brought a hand to her mouth to stifle a giggle. *If Owen could see him now*, she thought.

***

The fingers arrested their beat as a car pulled in behind the van. A hand moved towards the passenger seat before grasping a plastic freezer bag containing a computer memory stick. A glance in the wing mirror spotted someone moving towards the passenger door; the swiftness of the pace was in total contrast to that of the runner. With a click the door opened and a head appeared.

"You're late." The driver's voice was non-threatening, more an observation before the driver lifted the bag and held it out. The offering was eagerly taken. "They're on here?" No other words were spoken just a reassuring nod of confirmation. Within minutes the rear door to the van was opened and swiftly closed. Eyes glanced into the adjusted rear-view mirror to check the box was there. It was made of polystyrene, insulated, the type in which fish packed in ice might be transported. Fingers landed back on the wheel but now remained motionless. The car behind pulled out and moved away without drama. It slowed and turned into Silverdale Road before manoeuvring to leave as it had entered. Within a minute it had passed, a flash of the headlights signalling an acknowledgement.

The driver reached for the key. The engine turned but did not start, it usually needed three attempts before it would cough into life. Slipping it into gear, the van followed the same procedure as the car and soon left Granby Road.

Chapter 3

The high-pitched, blood-curdling scream brought some gasps from the guests still sitting at the tables, engrossed in the intensity of the interviews. One elderly lady threw her hand to her mouth knocking over a full glass of white wine, bringing more confusion to the gloom of the candlelit room. Cyril instinctively stood as his head turned in the direction of the scream. He watched Inspector Clapper dash from the room, his arm waving beckoning all to follow.

"Do come, but come quickly as we don't have a moment to lose!"

Cyril needing no encouragement, he was the first to follow glancing only briefly at Julie as she pursued a few yards behind; she held onto their glasses of wine as she could see he was fully engrossed in the melodrama that was unfolding.

The stream of guests followed in pursuit of the actors rushing down the corridor before turning into the library, some guests appearing more eager than others. The grandfather clock beat out nine chimes with a lethargy in keeping with its age but they were partially drowned by the sounds of many moving feet and the eager chatter. Cyril checked his watch, shook his wrist and checked again. He made a mental note that the clock was ten minutes slow. The group followed the Inspector's directions squeezing into the library before forming a circle around the prostrate body set before the hearth. A mass of blood seemed to have pooled on the back of the victim's white tuxedo. Lady Mary, the elderly dowager, one of the troupe of actors, sat away from the body, her walking cane to her left and she appeared to be supported by her nephew, Crispin Fitzgibbon. Her handkerchief was clasped closely to her face.

Clapper's Sergeant, Bob Sibson, quickly knelt by the body, his fingers moving to the side of the victim's neck. He was the first to speak once everyone was positioned and the chatter had died down.

"Lady Mary popped into the library, she heard a noise and here he was as you see him."

Crispin continued to console his aunt. "Is … he … dead?" His stuttered words were round and plummy as he held a glass of brandy to her lips.

The Sergeant removed his fingers from the man and the nod of his head confirmed it to be the case. "I'm sorry, there's nothing I can do for the poor man."

The Dowager began to sob and patted her eyes with a lace handkerchief.

Cyril glanced toward the window, the same window he had contemplated before dinner. The light skin of condensation gave a grey ghostly coat to the multiple square pained glass. His peripheral vision had caught a blurred movement, a face carelessly illuminated by the faint glow of a flashlight as it appeared only briefly. Whoever it was seemed to be looking in.

"The window!" Cyril's voice was raised and his arm shot in the direction. Instinctively more heads turned. He immediately became aware he had stolen the Sergeant's thunder who then shouted and pointed in the same direction. His cry was now an echo that highlighted the fact that he had been a moment too late. His face showed more than a degree of frustration at being beaten to one of his best lines. He got to his feet, paused momentarily, looked squarely in Cyril's direction and quickly left the library in pursuit. "Everyone, stay here!" His words, more an order than an instruction, seemed to be specifically directed at Cyril. Heeding the instruction, he turned and moved to the window, wiping the condensation with his hand, his swift action turning the opaque surface to running tears. In what illumination there was from the Hall's exterior lights, Cyril caught a glimpse of Sibson chatting with one of the actors, the butler, as they headed back to the main entrance.

On returning to the library Sibson pushed the butler into the room.

"Put up quite a chase but I was cross country champ at school." The Sergeant puffed up his chest and scanned the room as if seeking an accolade.

He soon received one. "Very well done, Sibson!" The Inspector took the butler by the shoulder and moved him into the light.

"He told me he was chasing some other fellow, says he caught him with his hand in the silver cabinet." Sibson raised his eyebrows as if the butler's story was a fabrication. "There's blood on his shirt too." Sibson pulled back the butler's black tail coat to reveal the blood stain.

The accused seemed flummoxed and out of breath but yet without a bead of sweat. It was then that Cyril looked at the butler's white gloves. They were unmarked.

"If there's blood on his shirt then why is there no trace on his gloves?" Cyril could not help but state the obvious.

Both the Sergeant and the Inspector turned. Each demonstrated his further frustration.

"Quite!" A false smile came to Clapper's lips. To Cyril it was more of a rictus. Clapper regained his composure. "Maybe he should explain his actions to me and this gentleman."

It was the butler's cue to speak his lines.

"I'd been clearing up after dinner. The maids had checked and dampened down the fire and as I came from the drawing room, I noticed what I assumed to be one of the staff. The lighting had been subdued so I stood in the doorway. It was then the person saw me. He was wearing a mask and held what appeared to be a cudgel and a sack. The silver cabinet was open. If I'm honest, I was quite shaken. I think I asked him to stop but the villain just laughed, it was muffled by his face covering. He reached for the bag and ran at me with the weapon raised. I lifted my tray to shield my head and whatever he held struck the tray and it flew out of his hand. He then struck me on the chest before fleeing. I naturally gave chase."

"Did you shout?"

"Yes, but the music seemed to drown everything."

The Inspector looked at Cyril and saw that he was about to speak. He raised a hand. "Sir, please let the police lead this investigation."

Julie squeezed Cyril's arm and giggled. "Easy tiger, it's

not for real."

Cyril turned, took the glass from Julie and downed the contents before leaving the room heading for the bar.

***

The polystyrene box sat on the table where it had lain since arrival. This was the first and a flutter of what seemed like a squadron of butterflies collided in the stomach bringing with it a contradictory fear and sensation of nausea. The same hands that had beat the rhythm on the steering wheel now clasped a mug of coffee. It had been the culmination of a great deal of work and focused determination to see it through but here in the box was the reward. It would soon begin.

***

DI David Owen sat with one foot on his desk, the other on the ground allowing an amount of sideways movement causing the chair to oscillate at will with only a slight squeak of protest. The swinging motion seemed to help him think. He studied the file that had arrived on his desk in the late afternoon. He glanced at the clock. He had a further three hours remaining. This late shift never suited him and it was rare that he took it, but the absence of staff and holiday leave meant it became a necessity. He glanced back at the file. *Bernard Jones, divorced, lives alone. At the address for about twenty years.* Owen swung his foot from the desk and stood before moving to the far wall where the street map of Harrogate was trapped behind plastic. He had an idea of the house's location but needed confirmation. Refusing to use the index he studied the maze of streets.

"Bingo!" His words rang clearly as he tapped the location with his finger, picked up a marker and drew a small red circle.

Harry Nixon put a mug of coffee on Owen's desk. "I believe *Flash* is at a Murder Mystery evening. Can't see him enjoying that one little bit."

Cyril had carried the sobriquet *Flash* throughout his career although very few dared use it to his face. It had been corrupted too. Some thought it was because he was always immaculately dressed, clean shaven and his shoes shone but they were misinformed; it had come from his name. Whilst training he had been called Gordon after James Gordon Bennett, the son of a publisher and an avid sportsman who created the Gordon Bennett Trophy for motor racing. This was of little consequence to Cyril as he was not too keen on his own Christian name feeling it was a tad old fashioned. Later, having been nicknamed, Gordon – which Cyril considered equally old fashioned – it was soon linked to Flash Gordon the space adventurer who first appeared in 1934. Flash seemed to stick.

"Had a call from Julie. She could hardly contain her delight as Cyril was fully involved, so much so he was ahead of the theatre. Thanks for the coffee." Owen tapped the map. "What do we know about Bernard Jones?"

"He's been missing for a few days. It's in the file. Didn't turn up for work, bakery on Market Place. Been there two years. They called it in after he failed to show or contact them. The manager had gone to his house but there was no response. His car was still on the driveway." Nixon moved towards Owen and took the file before leafing through. "Good work record. One black mark. Was reported by a temporary worker, a student, who claimed he touched her inappropriately."

"And did he?" Owen collected his coffee and took a sip.

"She left after her lunch break, didn't return. He denied it and it's reported the manager viewed the shop CCTV but there was nothing of significance. That's it, as I said, she just failed to turn up for work after lunch. And now he's followed suit."

"That's only a few days ago!" Owen looked at Nixon who responded with a nod, "He's divorced?"

"His partner left a few years back after becoming romantically attached to a regular client at the Harrogate hotel where she worked. She's now living in Madrid. Jones didn't always work in the bakery, he worked in hospitality like his ex-missus. He was a deputy manager and confided in his boss apparently saying they both worked anti-social hours and could often be ships that passed in the night. Not good when you're in your forties." Nixon winked at Owen. "He had a bit of a breakdown."

"Kids?" Owen drained the coffee mug rather matter-of-factly.

"Yes, a daughter, Kerry. She left home after finishing school. The mother had already gone. It was never reported at the time. Maybe he thought she was old enough to fend for herself."

Owen frowned putting two and two together but unsure if he'd reached the correct answer. "Aye, and maybe he didn't want her to stir a hornets' nest if she did return. Do we know the real reason? Seems unusual for a youngster to bugger off like but I suppose that depends on the home life. How close after her formal education finished?"

"A while after, and a reason? No, nothing as yet." Nixon rubbed his eyes. "It's been a long day. They've both been posted as missing on the various sites and added to the national computer as well as the risk assessments done according to procedure. Calculating the continuum of risk, Owen, one is low yet the daughter is classed as medium risk at present unless you look on the dark side."

"Do we know if the daughter is safe?"

"There's never been a report of her as actually being missing so we're now, in the light of the information received, assuming she's with relatives. Jones never reported when she left. We're in the process of chasing any information we can."

"Even though it's twisted, they're classed as missing and we should remember the three factors we must follow." Owen tried to remember the procedures off the top of his head. "Storm log created? Property search, hospitals checked and time scale for review et cetera? I think that's fairly close but it's worth a check."

"Done or in the process of."

"The girl, the one who made the accusation of inappropriate touching, worked here on a student visa. Eastern European if you class Turkey as such. She completed her studies. She's gone too. There's more to come about Jones but as yet we're still awaiting that information."

"Did she have an up-to-date student visa? Do we have contact addresses for her accommodation and her place of study?"

***

Cyril and Julie stood at the foot of the oak staircase. It was the widest he had ever seen. The heavy curtains on the first of the two landings had been drawn and a small chandelier produced a warm, ambient light giving a cosy and protective feel. The clock in the hall struck once. Cyril was about to check his watch but decided climbing the stairs was of greater importance. He was unsteady and to make matters worse he was working in the morning.

"The bloody nephew! My money was on that toff, Crispin Fitzgibbon, a character who was least like an apostle if ever I saw one. The more he spoke, the more I was convinced." Cyril shook his head, as his slurred pronunciation seemed to emphasise the touch of disappointment within his tone.

"That's good acting for you, Cyril. A lot of red herrings, too much red alcohol on your behalf and they had you kippered." She chuckled at her own pun but it swam over Cyril's alcohol-confused head.

"Did you know it took one man a year to renov ... reno ... repair this staircase?" He paused as he swayed whilst struggling with the sentence, trying to regain his equilibrium as he desperately grasped one of the ornate newel posts. "Marvellous job. Read about it in the booklet in our room."

After climbing to the next landing their room was in sight. Within five minutes of Cyril's head hitting the pillow he was asleep. The Murder Mystery evening had been more successful than Julie could have hoped. The busman had clearly enjoyed his holiday. Whether the same could have been said for the actors trying to keep one step ahead of

Cyril was only a matter of conjecture.

Chapter 4

Lifting the lid on the polystyrene box brought with it mixed feelings. There was an inner excitement, an anticipation and a tingle of nerves as if once the box was opened there would be no turning back.

"Would opening this bring emotional and physical curses on my already wretched life?" The words were spoken out loud to the empty kitchen but were immediately lost. The only other living thing was curled up and partially hidden in a confusion of bedding. "Whatever you do, remember to leave the lid off as you don't want to trap hope within." The story of Pandora's box was clearly within the thought process. The cat in the bedding stretched but quickly resettled.

With caution and apprehension, the lid was lifted, nothing mystical nor mythical seemed to rush out. It was tilted and then placed on the table. Sliding the box closer, the contents soon became clear to see. The face, pale, almost ashen, stared with blind eyes at the solitary light bulb held in the fitting directly above – the visage was almost statuesque. It was lighter than anticipated but the details were accurate. It brought a shiver alongside the memories as well as a bitter taste on the tongue. The only thing missing was the breath, the stale breath that had stung the nostrils throughout the many episodes.

Turning to the laptop the face staring back was identical to that held. The slight wrinkles, the imperfections were identical, only the eyes and ears were missing from the mask. A memory of seeing Dante's death mask immediately came to mind but this was different in one respect ... the person was still alive ... for now, that is, but the question was for how much longer?

***

The alarm brought Cyril swiftly to his senses. His head throbbed. He leaned and grabbed the phone whilst noticing a glass of water and a note.

Dinner out tonight!
Paracetamol next to the glass.
Have breakfast – it's paid for.
Have a good day. Car keys on the table.
Remember always Keep your eye on the Toffs!
Jx

Julie had been picked up from the hotel leaving Cyril the car.

Cyril let his head fall onto the pillow but only for a moment. He took a deep breath, grabbed the tablets and swung his legs out of bed. It was 8.15.

Closing the hotel room door, he tapped his jacket as he muttered, "Testicles, spectacles, wallet and watch." It was his routine. The broad staircase seemed different in the daylight. He paused to study a collection of four symmetrical Egyptian style stained glass windows set high in the huge windows' stone mullions. It was the richness of the contrasting blues and reds that struck him.

The ambience of the Hall's downstairs rooms had changed overnight; what was the bar was now the breakfast room. To his relief, classical music enveloped like an elixir to soothe his still throbbing head. The violins brought memories of his mother and with them an immediate comfort before he noticed the troupe of actors sitting round one of the larger tables. All smiled and nodded but continued eating.

As Cyril stepped through the front door of Goldsborough Hall he turned to walk to his car, the crunch of the gravel beneath his feet seemed to break the magical silence the morning offered. The sun hovered above a copse set within the Hall's grounds rendering the shapes to silhouettes. He watched a solitary female walking purposefully with a black Labrador around a field some distance away. His head throbbed distractingly.

Within thirty minutes he would be approaching Harrogate Police Station.

***

DI April Richmond watched as Cyril crossed the room. The occasional head leaned from behind a computer screen as he nodded to a number of his colleagues before turning to April. He smiled and formed a 'T' with his index fingers. She returned the gesture. The message had been received and understood; there was nothing sexist in the gesture it signified as it was she he wished to chat to.

Cyril was reading the details on his computer screen when she positioned the cup and saucer on his desk. To his surprise there was no slopped tea in the saucer. She also placed a packet of paracetamol with it.

"You look a little frail, sir. Good night?" She moved a chair and sat.

"Remind me to get Owen to watch how you deliver tea." Slipping his glasses from his nose onto his head he took a sip. "As my father used to say, April, 'You cannot be a man at night and a little boy in the morning', life goes on. Can you believe I failed to identify the killer? How embarrassing is that? The bloody toff did it." Shaking his head, he pointed to the computer screen. "Is that really for us – missing persons?"

"Missing persons." She emphasised the plural. "Normally no, unless they're found dead. However, we received an unusual communication through Crimestoppers. It's there."

Cyril dropped his glasses and scrolled down. "Grooming?" He turned.

"Look further. We received video footage from a paedophile hunting group calling themselves ShadowLink. It shows our missing man, Bernard Jones, being confronted. It's alleged that he'd arranged to meet a thirteen-year-old for sex but in fact it was a sting. As you can see, he protests his innocence but then breaks down under the shame and pressure. What surprised me more than anything, sir, was how dead his eyes looked."

Cyril watched the footage and nodded in response to

her observation. "Who the hell do these people think they are? I'm not in favour of vigilante justice neither is this police force."

"You'd be amazed how many of these groups are working across the country and not without results. They've brought a number of alleged paedophiles to the attention of the police I admit but … and it's a big but, the public might not see it as entrapment and believe spurious evidence that these groups remove a real threat from the streets."

"I don't subscribe to that theory, April, nor that of vigilante groups. A frightened man confronted by four big blokes and maybe a couple of females who seemed to do most of the talking might say anything, particularly if his emotional state is already in a state of flux simply out of fear."

"That's not all, sir. He was investigated at work for inappropriate sexual touching of a female employee."

Cyril quickly read further into the report. "No, he wasn't, April, that's conjecture as nothing was proven. The fact that she left immediately afterwards means nothing and her sudden absence could be argued in his defence." He tapped the screen at the relevant section of the report.

"If this group accosted him openly and threatened to expose him by uploading this video on social media, I believe he may have gone into hiding or has he been held against his will or even worse? We know suicides result from this kind of tactic."

April agreed. "After speaking with our Safeguarding Team, it's unusual for the video to come directly to us. It has, we believe, not been posted live nor is online to date and that's their usual way as well as involving the local police; naming and shaming and hoping for an arrest."

"That's my argument and that's why this force does not endorse these Online Child Abuse Activist Groups. We'll neither work with them nor have we mapped them or their areas of operation." He removed his glasses and tossed them onto the desk before taking the paracetamol.

Cyril continued. "There's more to this than meets the eye. I'm aware of the policy not to interact with groups but there's something in this that is totally at odds with hunter groups' standard procedure and rarely do we have missing persons linked unless they've taken their own lives."

***

The mask was still in the box. The room was empty, apart from the cat who seemed magnetically attracted to the human as they entered. It swirled around and between legs whilst 'talking' in a series of faint yet high-pitched pleas which grew in intensity as the cat's bowls were lifted, cleaned and filled; once back on the floor there came a return of both peace and silence.

"You're nothing but a fickle feline. You're lucky I like cats."

A mug was retrieved from the cupboard. Today was special, it had to be and it had to go smoothly.

Leaning into the box the mask was lifted out. The features were perfect, the imperfections, the facial hair and eye brows. The mask was brought up to face height as if looking into a mirror. "You bastard!" The words were uttered slowly and deliberately with every syllable emphasising the harboured hatred. "You will be found today, a clue, I will release a trapped secret, a secret I was forced not to tell."

Elastic was glued to the back of the surface to form a loop. One word, written in block capitals stood out in permanent marker against the grey-white of the material.

Once out of the house the air in the yard was fresh and had a cool nip to it even though the sun had penetrated the trees whilst changing the stone of the outbuildings' chameleon-like stone skin to the colour of dark honey. There was a beauty to the morning even on days like this, days that brought trepidation and uncertainty.

The van, parked in the yard, was anything but attractive. It was shrouded in a layer of dirt and mud. Some wag had taken the opportunity to finger write some chosen words within the grime on the side – *'Also available in white'*. It brought a smile. Opening the rear door, the box was slid into the back.

The traffic was lighter than anticipated apart from the usual crawl up near the theatre and the bus station but once past there, the one-way system ran more smoothly. At each set of red lights fingers beat a light rhythm on the steering wheel. Today it suggested a touch of nerves. The van turned left along Station Bridge and negotiated the Odeon cinema roundabout before entering the public carpark – the destination. The mask was collected from the box. It should now only take five minutes to complete the task, five minutes of apparent innocence to anyone observing, even though that was not the case.

Chapter 5

It was late in the morning when the discovery was made. The officer regaled the information to Owen.

"Nancy Doherty, a lady in her eighties, approached from Queen's Parade. She was calling on a friend whose apartment was situated within the old police station building, it was a weekly ritual. They met as the PLC, meaning the Prunes' Luncheon Club."

Owen looked up and frowned questioning the relevance of the last sentence but he said nothing.

"The false face, seen staring from the top of the post, stood out, incongruous and misplaced. Waiting for the traffic to calm she said she had moved over the crossing and paused to study it further. Within fifteen minutes three residents and Nancy Doherty stood discussing its merits. Barbara Ashcroft, the owner of the apartment, had photographed it and organised for its removal. It is, I'm informed, safe."

Owen thanked the officer who dropped the report on his desk before leaving.

Cyril had just finished a meeting with the Deputy Chief Constable, a man he had grown to respect since his promotion to the area. He was a colleague who had done it all, worked his way through the ranks and Cyril felt comfortable in his company. He too saw the need for a more intense concentration to investigate the disappearance of not only Bernard Jones, but also the student and Kerry Jones. He was under no illusion she would be on the radar after being absent for such a long period coupled with the uncertain circumstances of her absence.

Owen was still at his desk as Cyril moved through the open-planned office. His demeanour changed on seeing his boss and Cyril immediately recognised the instant frown.

"We've located Bernard Jones." Owen's tone was flat. "Here, see." He tapped the paper on his desk before shifting sideways on the wheeled chair giving Cyril a clear view of the computer screen.

"Are you taking the plod, Owen? It looks like a death mask."

"It's definitely his likeness. It's been suggested it's moulded from his face." Owen brought up the photograph of Jones and placed them side by side.

For a few moments Cyril said nothing as he looked at the screen. "A clever sculptor could create his features accurately in clay and then take the mould to create a negative to positive." As he was speaking his voice faltered with the uncertainty as he realised the complexity of the process needed. "Where was it found?"

"On the gatepost of the old Harrogate police station, now posh apartments as you know. It has been removed at the instruction of one of the occupants. It caused quite a stir. They were going to toss it in the bin but one of them thought there was something familiar about the features. They'd seen the post of our missing man on social media."

Cyril raised his eyebrows. "And the significance, I wonder? Why a mask? Why there? As a matter of interest when did it cease to be a police station?"

Owen quickly checked. "2012."

"Eleven years." Cyril frowned.

"The mask had been slipped over a stone urn that sits atop the post." Owen brought a photograph of the brick gateposts on *Street View* and zoomed in to enlarge the specific part. "Looks like a Greek urn with the small carving of a face at the centre."

"How high is that from the ground?" Cyril leaned closer. "Just move the image out again."

Owen reversed the zoom. Cyril counted the brick courses. "About thirty-five plus base and the stone plinth. Average brick height is, if my memory serves me correctly, about sixty-five millimetres so we're looking at the base of the urn sitting at ... two point three to two and a half metres. How tall are you, Owen?"

"Just over six foot four."

Cyril removed his phone and tapped a conversion into Google. "One hundred and ninety-three centimetres. You, with your arms stretched and standing on your toes might reach, but whether you could loop the cord of the mask over the urn securely is questionable."

"They stood on the fence?" Owen looked optimistically at Cyril as he pointed to the spiked wrought iron that sat at half the post's height and ran the length of the pavement.

"They? We're talking broad daylight on a busy road."

"Put on a fluorescent jacket these days and people

immediately think you're official. Set of steps too and no one would bat an eyelid. Northern towns and churches have lost more York stone paving slabs in daylight by that simple guise. 'Laying a new section of temporary path. These will be going back down …' These people are brazen and usually big and rough so no questions are asked. Job done!"

Cyril knew the theory to be accurate. "Do it right under their noses and they become blind. What else do we have? Any CCTV?"

Owen shook his head. "Nothing even from the camera on the electric gates. System shows nothing." He tapped his finger on the image of the mask. "On the inside of the face the word, *PANDORA* was written in marker pen."

Cyril rested his backside on the desk and rubbed his face. "Someone is either taking the proverbial or this is a subtle scattering of breadcrumbs to lead us back in time." He let his fingers search within the mug to the right of the screen and was rewarded with an Uncle Joe's mint ball. He unwrapped it and popped it in his mouth. "Or it's a cry for help." He let the refreshing mint flavour fill his mouth. "How did you interpret the word, 'Pandora', Owen?"

"A box that once is opened it releases stuff that cannot be returned nor the lid closed. I asked Grimshaw." He looked at Cyril as if expecting to be corrected. He was not disappointed.

Cyril shook his head. "Close but no cigar, my friend. It's an artifact in Greek mythology and not in fact a box. It's believed to be a large storage jar, not too dissimilar to those on top of the gateposts. The modern idiom can be interpreted as a gift that might appear valuable but is really a curse."

Owen scratched his head as he pulled a face. "So, what are you saying? Is Bernard Jones the curse or is it the mask?"

"If it's gone to Forensics let's wait, speculation at this stage is pointless. Has the person who found it been interviewed?"

Owen nodded. "People, sir. People all eager to give their two penn'orth."

***

Cyril sat with Julie. He let his finger run around the rim of the wine glass. "How easy is it to take a cast of someone's face?"

"Are they co-operative?" Julie rested her chin on her hands as if knowing where the conversation would lead.

Cyril shrugged his shoulders.

"If they were not it would be impossible. If they're co-operative or dead, easy."

"If they were unconscious, drugged?"

"Then it would be straightforward once the head was stabilised and set in a position. You're probably looking at about twenty to thirty minutes to get the job done depending on the material." She could almost hear his thought process. "That's only the start. You then have to use that as the mould to form the mask like the one you have. Negative and positive."

"DNA transfer?" Cyril sipped his wine.

"In the initial mould, yes. Probably facial hair even though the skin will have been covered with a releasing agent, Vaseline or some vegetable oil. Maybe nasal traces or fluid from the mouth. There's an additional consideration, the mould that touched the face would be similarly treated with a releasing agent, and if whoever did this for whatever sinister reason had any sense, they'd use some kind of bleaching agent too."

"Finger prints trapped within the material?" He knew he was grasping at straws.

"Gloves, Cyril, hooded coveralls. If this is planned, it's announcing to you that either your chap is alive and there's a story to tell, or it's stating he's dead. The place where it was left adds further credence."

There was a long pause as the food arrived. "One more question and the hangar door is closed for the night." Julie folded her arms as if forming a barrier.

"From the facial features, the expression captured maybe, could you as a pathologist say either way? Dead or alive when it was done?"

"I'd have to look very carefully and it would be pure conjecture." She unfolded her arms and picked up her cutlery.

Chapter 6

Owen sat in the Incident Room allocated for the investigation of both Jones and Gülen Köse, the missing student. Photographs of each and their known history had been identified and added to the whiteboard running down one wall, any potential links clearly highlighted; there were few. International official communications had identified known relatives of the young woman. They had not heard from her for well over a month but according to the reports that was not unusual, they had not seen her since she took her place at university therefore there was no reason to be alarmed.

"Bloody strange way for a family to behave. Daughter in a foreign country and they don't see her for years and only communicate on occasion. What does that tell you, April?"

"Independence, financial constraints, maybe considerable financial sacrifice." She paused. "Problems with home or personalities at home. There could be many reasons." She did not look up but spread the paperwork on the table.

"However, there are issues which might shine some light into her life," April continued. "United Kingdom Visas and Immigration shows Köse is at this time without a visa, it expired over four weeks ago. Records show she'd also paid the healthcare surcharge, and her tuition fees were up to date. She was in university accommodation in Leeds for the first two years and then, according to UNIPOL, went private – she was at this address." April pushed the details across to Owen. "Completed her studies, a three-year BA course in Art and Design. Not a particularly good grade but ..."

Owen looked askance for a moment at the details. "Turkish. Have you seen the fees for an international student? Over the three years that's some chunk of money to pay back. So why did she not just go home or reapply? Why was she working in Harrogate and how did she get employment?" The questions were asked in a whisper, as if rhetorical.

"She's running from something. Wants to stay but ... According to official figures the number of foreign nationals overstaying their visa has doubled in the last couple of years so we're talking ninety-five thousand who arrived with a visa but didn't leave. Obviously, they're not all students but the new ruling will mean they could face four years in prison if they are ever traced." A touch of cynicism was clear in Owen's voice. "Maybe for some that puts them between a rock and a hard place." April shrugged her shoulders.

"If she were illegally in the country ... I know that's strong but a fact ... why would you make a fuss about an alleged incident at the place you shouldn't be working?"

April shrugged her shoulders and exhaled. "Why indeed."

Owen turned to look at the photographs and details on

display.

"Art." Owen stabbed the paper with the marker pen. "Could she be responsible for the mask, either the making or the sculpting? She knew him, worked with him and allegedly left because of him."

April's expression suggested uncertainty. "She sculpted the face from which the mould was made? Possible, but getting the scale correct is not easy and what would be the reason. It's surely not because he touched her inappropriately. Considering your previous argument? She shouldn't even be here."

"Maybe, but she is and she's got a bloody degree in art. Scale and proportion should be part of her skill set. The reason?" Owen failed to answer but leaned closer to the board and studied her photograph then spoke out loud. "She's an attractive young woman. The work at the baker's was temporary. How temporary I wonder? Temporarily illegal that is. One or two days a week?"

"When required according to the owner. Mostly Saturdays but the occasional weekday to cover absence. The owner's not too happy either as he finds himself in a difficult position." April continued to shuffle the notes.

"So, she must have known Jones fairly well?" Owen was clearly puzzled by the disruptive nature of Köse's final year but his main concern at the moment centred on her name. "What's with the two dots over the 'u' and the 'o' in her name?"

"I checked that. You sound it like the one in 'oo'. At first, according to the boss, she always wanted to be called *Ghoul* but I assume it's not spelled that way and had a sinister connotation. Seems she carried that nickname at university too. Strangely enough, Owen, it means 'rose' in Turkish – somewhat different imagery! You can check the 'ö' yourself."

Owen wrote it on a Post-it note and added it to the board. "A phantom by name and now by nature! Uni friends? Lecturers? We've set the interview wheels in motion I take it. House search?" He glanced across at a number of still photographs taken from the video posted to Crimestoppers by the group calling itself *ShadowLink.*

"She never travelled home during her period of study according to immigration. Are we checking to see if and where she might have worked during the holiday periods?"

"Yes, Owen, it's in hand. Brian Smirthwaite is co-ordinating with colleagues from Leeds. Shakti has linked with the University. She's made contact with Köse's latest Academic Personal Tutor. From what she's discovered to date the tutor has worked with her since the midpoint of her final year. The previous tutor moved universities. It was a promotional career move," April added.

Cyril entered and the conversation stopped as he moved towards Owen. "Very little from Forensics to date but we know more about the mould and the mask. The word, *Pandora*, has been analysed and compared with Jones's handwriting but it's not a match; it was written using a black Sharpie. We await a comparison with Köse's handwriting. The mask is complex, not your simple Plaster of Paris. The negative mould we assume at present was taken directly from the face and made from a product called alginate. It's used for life casting. It doesn't damage the skin and sets quickly especially if heat is applied. Providing the nostrils remain clear, it's relatively simple to use. It's also very readily available and cheap. However, what was attached to the gate post is a product called PlastSil, it's a special effects prosthetic skin of safe silicone rubber. It's used to make life-like body parts, wounds for theatre and film."

"Does that mean we can disregard the idea of Köse sculpting the face?" April asked whilst tapping the word alginate into the computer.

"Not according to the boffins, they would need a negative so they'd use the same process only they'd not need a real person."

"There's a YouTube video showing life casting using alginate." April sent the images to the large wall screen. "You also need plaster bandages." She jotted down the list of items used. The video was only short. "The finished head is made from plaster."

"That would be the simple way, the process they use in schools and at home. The question is why did the perpetrator go to such lengths?" Cyril asked.

"Realism, accuracy life-like in death?" April brought up a photograph of the mask. "It's without colour but the features are detailed. It also has the texture of skin."

Cyril's mobile rang.

"Bennett." He threw the sheets he held onto the table.

April looked across at Owen and then at Cyril. "Jones?" She knew from his face to expect a body.

"Another video from the group calling itself ShadowLink. Another victim confronted. Another alleged thirteen-year-old groomed for sex. We also have another body part, not real, same material as the face. The video and photographs of the find should be available to view." Cyril pointed to the computer instinctively.

April worked her way into the system and retrieved the details. Owen leaned against the wall and watched the video. He shook his head on a number of occasions at those aggressively challenging the man insisting his guilt over his feeble protestations of innocence. It was a clear case of threatening and intimidating behaviour.

"The poor bugger's terrified. He can hardly put a sentence together." Owen turned to look at Cyril.

"Pause it, April."

She took the mouse and clicked.

"There's a profile caught briefly on camera about thirty seconds back. Female."

April scrolled along the frame bar stopping at the desired image.

Cyril moved closer to the screen. "Print that and get someone to run a comparison with known photographs of Gülen Köse. It's a hunch. Do we have a name for this person?"

"Asadi Kadare. He's an asylum seeker, Albanian, illegally entered the country. Presently staying in Clearview Hotel courtesy of the tax payer. He's one of eighty-three at that hotel. According to the video they suggest he's been there about three weeks and he's been communicating with what he thought was a child for the last week. A meeting was planned for today. He'd sent indecent images to her and requested she do the same." There was a hint of disgust in her voice.

"I take it they didn't call the police, the usual process?"

"As with Jones, no. Just sent the video through Crimestoppers but let's not forget they threatened to expose him as a paedophile," April responded.

"Any CCTV showing where this gathering might have occurred?"

"Checking. We'll know soon."

"Is Kadare still there or has he gone walkabout too?" Owen jotted down the name on a new section of whiteboard as he posed the question.

April shrugged her shoulders. "Awaiting news. According to this, the video was recorded yesterday but as yet we have no confirmation."

Within minutes they were looking at the photographs of the recently found body part. "It looks more like a waving hand. Where was it found?" Cyril demanded.

"On the gate post of a house at the start of Otley Road, just after Trinity Road. It comprises three apartments, so why there?"

"Otley Road?" Cyril looked directly at Owen and raised a finger. "I want a briefing later this afternoon. 16.00. I want Köse's university details, any findings from digital forensics after viewing the videos if possible. Location is critical and details regarding the profile of the girl. I need what Forensics have on the fake body parts, details from Smirthwaite's visit to her accommodation and Shakti's report of Köse's personal tutor ... And Owen, Otley Road, the connection, it's not rocket science. Clue!" He turned and left.

There was a silence for a few moments. "He's still mad that he didn't detect the killer on that Murder Mystery night. It damaged his copper's pride," said Owen.

Chapter 7

The clock on the wall showed 15.55. The officers requested to attend the briefing were chatting. Cyril entered, a notepad in hand. Unusually he did not smile but moved to the front and took a seat. The others quickly found seats. April was already primed at a keyboard. Looking around the room Cyril checked all the officers he had requested were present. He noticed Nixon and Park at the back.

“Thanks for your prompt attendance. We’ve got the green light from above to concentrate on the missing persons cases. As you know it was confirmed that we have four so far. However, the latest, Kadare, our illegal Albanian may well have just been frightened enough to go walkabout. It’s not uncommon for them to vanish, even when they’ve not been confronted by a group protesting guilt of paedophilia. The fact he was supposedly processed by border force should mean they have the necessary information to track him but they don’t. Against their human rights even though they came in illegally. Mark my words we’re making a rod for our own backs. As he’s missing and we’re very concerned for his wellbeing, I want his hotel room checking and I want his DNA. I also want any photographs, literature, IT equipment. If he thought he was meeting someone for sex or to take them back to the hotel, then most of what he owns will be in that room. If not, we fear for him." Cyril knew he was on thin ice and that rules were being stretched.

Shakti made a quick call.

"Let's go through this methodically. Seeing as you're here, Harry, tell us about Jones's early career," Cyril continued.

Harry Nixon did not stand. He opened his notes studying them for a moment. "Married Christine Pemberton in 2000, registry office and lived in Harrogate, initially renting a flat on Belmont Road. Career wise they both did well. She worked at The Burlington Hotel and progressed through various roles and he changed jobs fairly frequently, all in hospitality, finally settling in the role of catering manager at The Castle Hotel, Leeds. They bought a semi in Firs Crescent after three years. Daughter born 2002 but left home not long after her seventeenth birthday, that was 2019. They divorced in 2018."

"Do we know the reason for the divorce and the daughter's leaving?" Cyril asked.

"Christine had a dalliance with a regular client, foreign, lived in Madrid. She just took off. From what I've been able to establish from speaking to the neighbours, the relationship had been on the rocks for a while. The daughter, Kerry, was a bit of a handful from a young age and didn't seem to improve, hormonal I was told. Lots of banging of doors and shouting etc. It seems she didn't get on with her mother for some time before she buggered off with her foreign lover. Kerry was also left to her own devices when mother moved out and owing to the time demands on Jones at work. There's a suggestion the family just imploded and crumbled. School reports confirmed she was a bright and attentive student but noticed a slip towards the end of her studies. She left and didn't complete her final exams."

"Since 2019?"

"Jones handed in his notice at work before Kerry left, he'd realised things were going from bad to worse. The commute and the hours were destroying what family he had left. He got a number of temporary jobs until finding his present position. It seemed to make no difference, she still left. According to the neighbour, it nearly broke him."

"Have we tracked Christine Jones or has she reverted to her maiden name?"

"In the process. We'll be interviewing her with the help of our Spanish colleagues over the internet tomorrow at eleven."

"And what of Kerry?" Cyril was ready to make a note. "I'm becoming increasingly uncomfortable professionally with this."

Nixon shook his head. "Ongoing, it's as if she vanished in a puff of smoke."

"Vanished! Harrogate's becoming the Bermuda bloody triangle all of a sudden." Cyril frowned, thanked Harry and turned to Shakti. "What do you have on Köse from her personal tutor?"

"The tutor's a Mrs Samantha Brownley. She only worked with Köse in her final year and that proved more difficult for her than expected – her words – 'Like treading on egg shells most of the time'. Köse didn't miss lecture sessions as she was bound by her visa to attend, it was mandatory but appointments with Brownley were rather cavalier; they were what was referred to as *open* and so not within the registration process. From reading between the lines, things started to break down with the previous personal tutor but as you know he left, moving universities. If necessary, we can make those specific enquiries as and when, there may be a link." Shakti looked up briefly as if seeking Cyril's approval before continuing. She caught his nod of the head. "There were a few concerns over her final year show, but not enough to sink the ship. It concerns the exhibition of her chosen art work for assessment. It was explained to me that it was thought she'd changed direction, not only creatively but as a person. She'd become more insular and this was reflected in her work and in the general presentation and style. It was as if she'd suddenly became fascinated by collage and the work was ..." Shakti looked down at her notes and read from them. "According to her tutors and I'll quote, 'An insidious corruption of style and technique allowing the development of a deep and worrying undertone of sexual content that seemed not only incongruous to her usual artistic style and moral values but also to the planned direction of her work when considered as a whole over the previous study time.' And as I said she had grown more insular too."

"That's some review! Did they guide her or try to understand the reason for the sudden ..." Nixon struggled for the correct word, "diversion?"

There was a long pause until Cyril broke the silence.

"The final year for any student can be difficult, either from the pressure to succeed at such a vital time in life, through peer group pressure whilst planning and co-operating with those exhibiting too or the unseen, strained relationships not only personal but also with family. They all mix to make a heady cocktail that will bring stress and poor quality of thought. Being an international student may possibly create even more pressure. Further to your earlier point, Shakti, international students have, I believe, to clock into every session for reasons linked to their visa. That can also seem oppressive." Cyril looked around the room reading the faces of his colleagues.

Shakti continued.

"I requested photographs of her degree show and the brochure or catalogue they produce." Shakti passed a computer memory stick to April. The images appeared on the large wall mounted screen and although Cyril showed immediate interest, the same could not be said for most of the group. Shakti slid the copy of the show's brochure across to Cyril. "According to her main tutor, the students work towards their show with other chosen peers, they work co-operatively to select work that demonstrates their ability as well as complementing the collective pieces. It's a critically important part of the course as a good show links them and their studies with the world of work, galleries, collectors and art journalists. It was at this stage Köse's relationships with her tutor and more so her personal tutor seemed to dip to its nadir. To help qualify this, records show that earlier in her course she was always a regular at her personal tutor drop-in sessions, eager it could even be said, but then this became erratic until it stopped in the final year."

"Stopped, like falling off a cliff?" Owen asked whilst

twiddling with his pen.

"I asked that very question. No, not initially but a gradual failure to comply. With her new tutor she met only when absolutely necessary."

"What do we know about her first personal tutor … type of relationship?" Smirthwaite asked. There was an undertone in his question.

"Male, Dr Callum Shaw. He'd been at the university for nine years. Left, it was a promotional move. He had a very good record." She smiled as she answered, understanding fully the insinuation Smirthwaite had wrapped within the question.

"Has anyone from the teaching staff kept in touch with her through Linkedin and the like since the course ended?" Owen responded.

"They'd tried but nothing returned."

Cyril pointed to the screen. "I think I'm correct in saying that during the show students timetable themselves to be present when its open to the guests and the public. How was Köse at this point?" Cyril's pen was at the ready to note the answer.

"Neither reliable nor co-operative according to her Personal Tutor."

"Boyfriends? Girlfriends?" Cyril continued to probe.

"I have a name and contact. It's being followed up."

Cyril leaned back in his chair and interlocked his hands behind his head and chuckled. "I note art speak continues to be as pretentious as ever. In Köse's description of elements of her work she suggested they are evocative …" He paused. "Why?"

There was only one response and that was from Owen.

"Because they make me think of a dog's bloody dinner and not a particularly appetising one?"

"According to Köse, 'because they evoke'!" Cyril raised his eyebrows and removed his hands as if in despair. "'Dog's dinner', right. Let's move on. Chase the first personal tutor and the boyfriend." He turned to Owen. "Residents from the old police station. Anything new? Forensics?"

"Just the report from Nancy Doherty, the woman who first saw the face. We've requested dashcam footage for the whole of that day in the hope we catch someone on some steps or balancing on the fence." He sounded extremely pessimistic. "Nothing from the public request for witnesses on the usual channels. The Forensic results are in the file for both the face and the hand."

"Videos taken by the paedophile hunters?" Cyril's response was eager and abrupt.

"Interestingly," Owen continued, "although we see the suspected perpetrators, still images of the alleged as well as photographs sent to the girls displaying their genitals, an important point here, we never see a full frontal. There's no proof that image A belongs to image B – they could be copied from anywhere, internet's full of it if you look. If they did show full frontal nudity including Jones's head, they might be deepfakes. I learned that it's a portmanteau of the words 'deep learning' and 'fake'. Putting a head and face onto another body. The software is so good it's difficult to differentiate between what's real and what's not! It's used extensively in the porn industry to add the face of a celeb. It's fake news on steroids!"

Cyril shook his head. "It's depravity at its very worst.

Everyone needs to be a Doubting Thomas these days and see things for what they really are rather than being manipulated, fraudulent and perverse."

"Indeed. However, we've just tracked the locations where both were filmed. The first with Jones is at the end of Stone Rings Lane. The road bleeds away to a footpath. It's not far from his home, and from what we understand from Harry Nixon, it's a regular walking area for him, but maybe not any longer." Owen informed the group.

Harry interjected. "Used to take a neighbour's dog walking when his wife left him, the same neighbour told me that it took his mind off his troubles. When the dog died, he continued the walks alone."

"It was clear from the video that the group ShadowLink believed he was meeting the girl there."

"Wife goes, daughter goes and the dog dies. He must have killed a priest in a past life!" Smirthwaite added with a chuckle that was not reciprocated.

Owen continued. "Asadi Kadare, we believe was confronted just off Hornbeam Park, on the bridleway, it's not far from his allocated hotel and it has to be said that area is possibly too open for the liaison of the nature they were suggesting but he may have been heading somewhere or planning to take her back to his room. We need to keep an open mind. More work is being done on the profile of the female you spotted, sir, but there's nothing conclusive as yet. They're using their magic to investigate in greater depth."

On completion, Owen stood and pointed to the photograph of the prosthetic hand placed on the top of a gate post. "Rocket science you said?" He looked directly at

Cyril. "That's what you said about the location." He shook his head. "Sorry, but I've no idea to what you were referring!"

"Anyone answer?" Cyril looked at each face in turn but either received a shake or a definitive 'no'. "The building was once the home of Michael Rennie's mother; it was also where he died suddenly." Cyril looked round again at the same blank expressions of his young colleagues. He personally had never seen the television programmes, he still did not own a television, and he certainly was not born when they were shown but he had by chance heard the story. "The Rennies and their son, Michael, a Bradford born actor, who was probably most famous for his role as Harry Lime in the television version of *The Third Man* and with that, there's an idea to conjure with. He's a man who in the original story disappears, believed dead but ... However, that's not all, the house became the first forensic laboratory in the North East. It was where the well-known expert Professor Angela Gallop started her career. She corrected, through her dedicated work, some serious miscarriages of justice." A number of people in the room suddenly showed signs of recognition. "The location could have relevance to the case or is it like the previous location purely chance? That degree of coincidence does not happen by accident."

"So, you believe knowledge of this Harry Lime chappie is meant as a deliberate clue linked to one or more who've gone missing?"

"Never leave anything to chance. Seize every opportunity to find answers to the questions and by doing that we come closer to solving the crime."

There was a long pause as Owen raised a finger whilst

looking puzzled. “Why rocket science?”

Cyril laughed. “Sorry, that was a tad cruel. The actor playing Rennie’s sidekick in the TV series was a chap by the name of Jonathan Harris and he was famous for being a lead actor in the programme, ‘Lost in Space’. Appropriate in a way – Lost.”

“For someone who purports to not watch or own a television you seem to know an awful lot of TV trivia.” Owen winked at the group.

“Secular knowledge, my dear Owen, secular knowledge. Comes from reading and keeping abreast of what goes on in the town in which you live.”

Chapter 8

Leaving the police station early, Cyril extended his walk along Otley Road. Rather than cut across The Stray, his usual route, he continued before pausing in front of the gate of a large stone detached property. There was no sign to show the hand had been attached to the post nor that it had once been a hub of Forensic Investigation for the north east area. He slipped a mint from his pocket to satiate the craving he still had for his electronic cigarette. *Is someone telling me something or are they playing a game of mischief?* he thought whilst moving onto the gravel driveway. He had read before leaving the station that as well as the main building being the Forensic lab the old stables and coach house to the rear were used for ballistic investigation. He contemplated when it was last used.

He was still ten minutes from home. A brisk walk around the edge of The Stray would bring him onto West Park and soon the ginnel that separated West Park from Robert Street. Its narrow confines seemed lighter than usual and yet the gloom still seemed allied to a breeze that always channelled its way through the gap and could often be as cutting as a sharp knife. Once through, however, the welcome sight of home lifted his spirits or was it the thought of a glass of Black Sheep Ale?

***

There was little to report the next morning from those working the case overnight and that brought further frustration. Nixon was standing in front of Owen's desk when Cyril approached from his office. "Just interviewed Christine Jones over the web, Bernard's ex, she was in the company of the Spanish police. She's neither seen nor heard from Bernard nor her daughter, Kerry, in over six months, maybe even longer. She's aware that she'd left home but according to her that was always going to be on the cards."

"What the bloody hell does that mean?" Cyril shot back angrily. "Why was it such a fait accompli?"

"Kerry was the first to spot her mother's affair. She came home from school unannounced and she then threatened to tell Bernard unless ..."

"Blackmail?"

Nixon avoided answering as he was eager to tell them more. "That wasn't all. There's a bigger bombshell ... Kerry isn't Bernard's child." There was a long pause. "He knows now. Let's say it was a parting gift she presented to him when she left. Another dalliance earlier on in their relationship."

Owen contemplated the word *dalliance* and raised an eyebrow at the usage. "An affair! Bloody hell!" His words were but a whisper but they were loud enough for all to hear. "What a secret to conceal, deliver and then bugger off! No wonder the poor sod was all over the place."

"Their daughter, Kerry, what did she threaten when she held the upper hand over her mother and when was she then told that he wasn't her father?" Cyril grabbed a chair and pulled it towards the desk. He sat on it the wrong way round and leaned on the backrest.

"The mother managed to keep her silenced for a while as she told her that the 'liaison' she'd witnessed was a one-off, a foolish mistake, and that she was sorry. She admits to giving in initially to Kerry's demands but the girl became too demanding and besides Christine Jones was still knocking off the guy when he was over in the country."

"The antithesis of good parenting." Cyril's cynicism was very clear within his tone as he glanced at Owen and then at the framed photograph of his son, Christopher, positioned proudly on the desk. "Parenting, bringing up kids, Owen, is something no one is trained for, there's no handbook, there's just the experience from your own upbringing and the application of a mass of common sense and love. I've not had kids but I hope I would always consider their wellbeing over all else, particularly my own. Good parents are selfless."

"So where is she?" Owen responded. "Four people, two from the same family have just disappeared."

Shakti Misra entered in a hurry. "We have a 101 report that a man matching Bernard Jones's description was seen with a young woman or a girl a few days back on the footpath at the end of Stone Rings Lane. The person had been concerned at the time as the couple appeared to be having, 'a bit of a row'. It was only when the faces of those missing appeared on the local news report did the potential severity of what they'd witnessed become apparent. And as an aside, the witness also announced that our link with the public in the form of the telephone contact number 101 isn't fit for purpose and she said that she was very close to hanging up."

"Don't we know it, Shakti! We're going out there. Do you have an address for your witness?" Cyril asked as he stood, took her by the elbow before turning to Owen. "I want the people from ShadowLink found and questioned. I also need to talk to Köse's boyfriend. Why is it taking so long? I also want Jones's house searching. Laptop, computer, a full sweep."

***

The small detached house looked relatively well maintained which was more than could be said for the front garden. The skeletal remains of what was once a rockery, once someone's pride and joy, was still partially visible but nature had taken back what man or woman had tried to tame. The collection of random conifers, bordering the plot, were overgrown in both height and width as if trying to match the many pine trees that ran along the road, casting deep shadows across the concrete driveway. To the opposite side and in total contrast was a neighbour's immaculate lawn.

Shakti checked the house number against her notes. "This is it. I called and she should be expecting us."

The lace curtain twitched at the front window as they closed the car doors and continued to do so as they approached the front door. It was then drawn back fully revealing the face of an elderly woman. The curtain fell and within minutes the door was opened until it snapped on the security chain.

"Mrs Peacock? I'm DC Misra and this is DCI Bennett." She held up her ID. "You rang 101 and spoke with control about seeing a man you later noticed on the local television news. We're grateful for your call and I know it can be tedious to get through. May we come in?"

There was a pause and the door was closed gently and the chain removed before opening fully.

"You can never be too careful here particularly living on a road that leads to the footpath. We used to have a number of garage and sheds broken into, push bikes mainly and gardening tools stolen and I have to say, Detective Chief Inspector, your lot did nothing."

Cyril glanced at the garden to his left and raised an eyebrow.

"I do hope I'm not wasting valuable police time … they say that on the detective programs on the telly a lot. You've come about the man with the girl?"

"Before we come in could you show us where you saw them, please?"

Shakti and Cyril moved to either side of the door and she stepped out, appearing more agile than either had imagined and moved towards the road.

"Just at the bottom, this road's a bridleway so we get all sorts. There's a gate to the right, it's where the road proper ends and there's a style through the wall allowing access to another footpath which takes you over the fields. If you continue down to the left the path takes you to Burn Bridge but I suppose you know that." She smiled, looked at both officers and went back to the house. "Tea?"

Shakti looked at Cyril who followed her in. "No thank you, not today. That must be quite a busy spot, the road end what with walkers and such like."

They entered and Mrs Peacock led them to the lounge.

"Summer more or when the weather's fine. A few pop down there at night, in cars. Nothing wrong with a bit of romance, we used to call it a bit of slap and tickle but that's been simplified to one word slang, but it's what they leave. Quite disgusting!" She pulled a face. "Let me tell you about the man and the lass. I'd walked my dog, she's in the back. She'd be all over you if I let her in. We don't go far as we are both ladies of a certain age. There were two cars parked ..."

Cyril interrupted. "What time was this?"

"I'd say just after seven in the evening. It was still light although the dusk comes early with all the trees. I don't go out in the dark now if I can help it. There was no one in the cars and only them, the couple. I saw him first and he was wagging a finger at what looked like the hedge and then I saw the girl. It was then he saw me and he froze for a moment, took the girl by the arm and moved further down the path. I stopped where I was and watched for a few moments but they continued until out of view."

"Was it the man we posted as missing?" Shakti asked.

"One of them from the picture, yes. There were two men, the other was Albanian if I'm not mistaken and younger and there was a young woman too. Careless of you to lose three at the same time." She chuckled bringing her hand to her mouth as if she had practised the line. "Seeing them had worried me but I heard no more and put it to the back of my mind. It was only when I saw the appeal that it brought it back."

"The girl. Can you describe her?" Cyril leaned forward, his hands clasped on his knees.

"I didn't really see her face much, just a flash as he turned her away so quickly but she was short, you might say, child-like. I remember he kept looking at me and then they disappeared. I got this feeling that something wasn't right. I've lived here a long time and I've walked there many times and met many people … but on this occasion …" She paused and wrapped her hands around her arms and appeared to shudder. "I felt very uncomfortable."

Cyril removed a sheet of paper from his pocket, it contained a number of photographs of men. "Can you see him on here?"

She collected the sheet and tilted her head as if reading through the lower portion of her varifocal glasses. She pointed immediately to Bernard Jones.

"And the cars. Do you remember anything about them?"

She thought for a moment before turning to Cyril. "I think one might have been a van."

Chapter 9

Cyril lifted his phone and began to video concentrating specifically on the area described by Mrs Peacock where the road met the track. A car was parked facing the hedge. He put his hand on the bonnet but it was cold. Across the field on the footpath a couple walked with a dog. It seemed a busy place contradicting the initial idea of solitude the countryside close to the built-up area instilled.

"If you were meeting a girl, an underaged girl, why here? You have houses there with windows overlooking, dog walkers, horse riders, probably joggers and maybe even Uncle Tom Cobley. In other words, it seems busy."

"It's five minutes from his empty house. Meet, check the waters and then make a decision," Shakti replied. "He'd be anxious and here, this location affords many opportunities of leaving if anyone comes … and unfortunately for him they did."

Cyril tapped a pencil against his teeth. "He finds out how compliant is the girl? Decisions are then made." Cyril mumbled seeing the possibility.

Shakti nodded. "If she's not or if you're disturbed you have a number of exit strategies as you say, four in fact. I would imagine he would hope to take her home and maybe he did so but not immediately."

"This is also the location in which he was stopped by ShadowLink. The sting, the setup. We know that happened after the date Peacock saw him. They obviously knew he came here, maybe they knew he walked here with the neighbour's dog. Maybe he did invite a girl, underage or not on more than one occasion. Did they have that information? He believed he was inviting a girl that time too but he was in fact communicating with the hunter group."

"It could have been the first time and this witnessed meeting was innocent." Cyril turned and took in the scene before moving back towards the car. "Could it even have been Kerry?"

***

"There was nothing. The Jones house was remarkably tidy. No computers, tablets or phones. Not even a television but a number of shelves full of books." Grimshaw's tone conveyed his surprise. "I've lived on my own after splitting up and I could never keep my home like that." He put a couple of framed photographs onto Cyril's desk. "Kerry."

Cyril picked up the first. A teenager stared back but had the appearance of being older. She was dressed in white and held a tennis racquet. To her right was Bernard Jones, the height difference was marked when compared to some other players standing nearby.

"I take it we don't know when this was taken?" Cyril handed it to Grimshaw.

"She left in 2019 so I'd guess on or before that."

"Tennis clubs in Harrogate? Which one's that?" Cyril picked up the second photograph, it was the same girl but younger, looking very excited. He put down the frame. "Look behind them Brian. It was taken just down the road."

"Right, yes, Harlow Hill water tower. The tennis courts are there."

Cyril checked on the computer. "Plantation Road. Contact someone at the club. It's urgent. I want to know when that was taken. It was obviously some club event. Check also when they were last members."

***

Derek Coulson sat in the office at the university and stared out of the window with little to no focus on the outside world. He had felt a degree of trepidation after receiving the call from his personal tutor and it had not receded, in fact it had grown to a nausea that he was just managing to control. The words police and Gülen Köse in the same sentence did not sit well. He thought about the last time they had been together and the final moments of the disagreement played out again and again in his mind's eye.

The door opened and DC Stuart Park walked in. Derek's tutor leaned in, introduced them but did not follow Park. "May I get you gentlemen a drink? Coffee?"

Derek had stood as Park entered; his face flushed slightly.

"I'd love a coffee, white and no sugar." Park smiled at the tutor. "Thank you."

Derek shook his head. "No thanks, I'm fine. I have water." He held up the bottle.

The door closed. “Thanks for seeing me.” Park took his electronic pad and placed it on the table as both sat. “For the report.” He tapped the pad. “We’re trying to locate Gülen Köse and we were informed you two were going out together at the end of her time here?”

“That’s not altogether true.” His voice quivered slightly with a degree of uncertainty.

The door opened and the coffee was placed on the table. Park took the mug and sipped it allowing Derek to continue.

“Up until about the last few months, maybe longer, we saw little of each other before her final show. We just finished or to be accurate she’d had enough. We’d also had a row as her degree show was getting closer. She was being a total arse.”

Park nearly lost the mouthful of coffee. The statement was just so matter of fact. “Please explain.”

“She’d changed from when I first met her, her outlook and general demeanour, if that’s the right term, maybe I should say it was her outlook on all things that shifted. It was like the fun had gone. At first, she was alive and enthusiastic and bloody talented. She was a skilled draughtsman, great accuracy, her life drawings were exceptional. That’s where we met, that class. Over the course of maybe eleven months, she changed. Initially it was a slight dip but then she picked back up. Her personal tutor was a great help I remember. She’d often pop along to talk things through with him. But then ...” He pulled a face that demonstrated deep thought. “… she became worse!”

“Can you say how and why this change happened?” Park continued to take his notes.

"Little things. She'd fail to turn up or she'd come very late when we'd made specific plans. Didn't stay over as often, in fact she didn't stay over at all later on, she seemed to become sexually indifferent. It was as if something was bothering her. She'd snap, pick fault and we'd end up rowing. It was the smallest of things that would be the spark. More importantly her work changed too and there was a gradual decline in its quality and content as far as I was concerned. I tried to offer guidance but that seemed to make matters even worse."

"Can you be specific about the change in her work and therefore her?"

Coulson paused and his facial expression changed. "Her work became darker and she concentrated more on collage." He laughed with incredulity and shook his head. "She was so talented. Christ, even developing bloody collage when she had such a fine artistic talent it was a sin! Her artistry became more casual and less skilled with an unusual sexual content, which contradicted the norm. As I said, she became cold and distant and not open to advice or comment. At this point all physical contact stopped. Naively, I thought she just needed time. Strangely, I thought she was bringing to her work problems from her past, maybe from her childhood. She spoke little about that period in her life."

Park looked up and waited. "What in your opinion was the reason for the sudden change?"

Coulson sipped some water as he looked out of the window before turning back to at Park; there was an anger in his action.

"To be honest? My gut feeling was that she was having

an affair, sorry, another relationship and had been for some time."

"Do you know who?"

Coulson shook his head. "We were drifting apart. I tried to talk to her about her work, tried to get her back on track when she started with her new direction of work well before and during her final show. This might sound weird but it was as if she were simply a shell. Her inner fire, her spark and emotions seemed to have been extinguished and believe me, at first, I felt truly bloody guilty, as if it were possibly my fault."

"In the time you were together did she ever talk about her family?"

"As I said, not a great deal. She never had photographs of them in her room. As far as I'm aware she never went back home. Travelled in the UK during the breaks but home to Turkey? I don't think so."

"When was the last time you met with her?" Park finished his coffee.

"The final day of her show I went in to see it, had friends who were also showing in the same exhibition and it's always good to be supportive. We all arranged to meet afterwards, she agreed but she didn't turn up. From what I heard from the group she'd been a total pain in the arse from start to finish. She's been neither seen nor heard of since. I've been to her place but nothing, even tried contacting her on social media but nothing."

"Mobile?"

"I'm assuming she's changed it as I've no contact with the number I have. To be honest with you, I thought she'd gone back home owing to her visa. I know she didn't extend and it will have expired by now."

Park read through the statement he had written, made two changes and Coulson signed it.

"If you do hear from her, I really need to see her." Park gave his contact card. "Or if you hear someone else has seen her ... Thanks for your time."

"Is she safe?" Coulson put his hand on Park's arm. There was real concern in his voice.

"To be honest, we don't know. People can just disappear but from what you've said she was clearly not the woman you thought you knew. That, Mr Coulson, brings with it a concern."

***

Grimshaw intercepted Cyril as he left a finance meeting and from the look on his face things had not gone well.

"Balance sheets never make fascinating reading. I take it money comes before fighting crime, sir?"

Cyril raised his eyes as if looking for inspiration. "The famous saying comes to mind, Dan, "'You can't make a silk purse from a sow's ear without spending on a good surgeon.'"

It was Grimshaw's turn to frown. "Never heard that ..."

"Made up but you get the idea. Risk assessments, budget constraints, staffing, overtime, Forensics are as important as detective work. We're hobbled before we start." He held up a thick file.

"Tennis. The Jones family were members of the club since she was very young. Junior coaching and according to the secretary the girl, Kerry, was outstanding. Often played against the older lads and would beat them. The photograph was taken after the club's annual competition. She won the Campbell Trophy. Her father encouraged her. He played but only social tennis. His wife didn't play. Their membership ceased at the end of the 2019 season. Never been back. There were a few photographs on the club wall and Kerry played in a local league. Sad such talent should wither on the vine because of parental strife."

"From what I recall she was not an easy child. Maybe pretentious and self-centred. Thanks, Dan."

Dan immediately left as Cyril's phone rang. "When?"

"Late yesterday." Shakti continued as Cyril put the call on speaker. "It's just coming in for some reason. It's now known that a Gina May Thomas aged sixteen had arranged to meet a person she believed to be a boy of eighteen she'd been chatting to online after school. We do know she left school and from CCTV and from some reliable witnesses, we know she went towards Hookstone Beck or the Hookstone Trails. At that time in the afternoon, we know the area would be busy and the main road is usually full of students ..."

April came in mid-way and moved to a desk.

"Coach Road? The Coach Road runs from Hookstone Drive, Hookstone Road and Oatlands Drive starting at the crossroads, they're controlled by traffic lights. There are, as you know, two schools in the vicinity and so at the end of the school day a considerable number of students are knocking about." Cyril added and looked over to April.

April brought up Google maps and honed in on the area. "The Coach Road runs towards Hookstone Beck. There's a bridleway linking with Hornbeam – it's where

Asadi Kadare was intercepted." She turned to look at Cyril who moved closer and traced the route with his finger.

"Why do they fill hotels with these people, hotels that are situated so close to schools? Nobody knows who the hell they are."

April stood back. "I'm sure there are many genuine refugees but I understand fully your concern and also that of the locals. This fear, this uncertainty is what feeds groups like ShadowLink to believe they are some kind of good Samaritan and I guess there are many who'd subscribe to their way of thinking. Asadi was intercepted by the hunter group two days before the girl went missing. The parents only knew there was a problem when she didn't go into school the following morning; the school telephoned to ask about her absence."

"Let's try and get some perspective. He's an asylum seeker, he has little money, certainly no car and yet he has the means to communicate with her. From what we saw on the video we know his spoken English is good and we assume too so was his use of the written, as according to ShadowLink they communicated through WhatsApp texts and some were recorded messages." Cyril's frustration was clear. "Where did he go after he was accosted and videoed? We know he went back to the hotel but left shortly afterwards. It's in their security log. How was he, have we interviewed those who keep this log and how accurate is it? We also need to talk to his fellow refugees."

"There's a need for translators." The financial implication had a bearing. "The security people we can interview. On a positive note, the parents have got friends and neighbours out looking for her in the area."

Cyril let his fingers walk the map on the screen again before tapping a set position.

"I want a full search of the bridleway and the possible tracks off. There's a path crossing the railway line leading from Hornbeam Business Park so there's also the cutting to either side to search. There's also a good deal of empty land in the vicinity. Remember at that time of day it's light, it's a popular route for dog walkers and the like." Cyril continued to follow along the route from where she had last been seen and stopped at the spot where Kadare had been intercepted. "Let's not forget it was on a similar bridleway that Jones was last seen with a girl or young woman."

Cyril looked at April as he emphasised both names insinuating a possibility. "Jones and Kadare? Jones was in hospitality, knew many in the hotel trade. Could they be involved?"

April rested her head on her chin. "In hotels, yes, but the hotels housing migrants have their own staff. The original staff are often sacked or to be more politically correct, made redundant which amounts to the same thing as they've lost their livelihoods."

"If Kadare was involved there are a few things to consider. Firstly, if he were intercepted the day or two before why would he dare contact someone and if so, why Gina May Thomas? He'd no idea if she were another plant, another sprat to catch a mackerel. Would he take that risk? Secondly, if he did a runner why would he be back here? There's a greater chance of his being seen. What do we really know about him?"

April tapped into the computer. "Albanian, came from a town of Lushnjë in the county of Fier. Quite a small population. We know little else other than what we saw on the video. Aged about twenty-four but you can never tell. We're making enquiries – Albanians taking the illegal, costly and dangerous route usually have a past they wish to keep hidden."

"Why cross the Channel in a small inflatable unless you've got something to hide, a criminal past?" Cyril shook his head. "Something is beginning to smell wrong. What with a rubber face and hand obviously moulded from one of the missing and then another female goes off without trace, now Thomas and Kadare. Tell me this is not a beer induced dream, April."

Chapter 10

The van was parked in the usual location. It was some way off dusk. The lights set within The Stray were still not illuminated, but near the trees the early evening had delivered a premature depth to the shadows. The same dirt still layered the paintwork as if helping to blend it with the failing light. The driver's fingers beat the repetitive pattern on the wheel, it was instinctive; the tune on the radio bore no resemblance to the rhythm. The wait had been longer than was promised but there was nothing to be gained by becoming frustrated or angry. Considering the time of day, it was what it was. A blue car passed before the red tail lights flashed, the vehicle slowed and turned higher up the road before returning more slowly. As it approached the headlights flashed once before it pulled up behind. Within a moment the van door opened and the familiar polystyrene box was deposited before the door was slammed shut. A hand tapped the roof, a quick signal comprising two bangs. It echoed inside. Watching through the wing mirror, fingers rested, still motionless as the car pulled away. The van followed shortly afterwards.

***

The ring tone on Cyril's phone sounded just as he was polishing his shoes. The aroma of something cooking drifting from the kitchen had filled his nostrils as well as his thoughts since his arrival home. The beer was on the side. It was a change from his usual. He had poured a Black Moor from The Goose Eye Brewery. The label had caught his attention when out shopping and the ale did not disappoint. Little did he know the name would, within minutes, be prophetic. Julie was reading. He answered the call in his usual curt fashion.

"Bennett." He held up the shoe to the light inspecting the mirror-like finish to the leather as he listened. "Shit! Send a car. Fifteen minutes. Do we know whom?"

Julie turned.

"A body, male. I've been expecting a corpse. It had to come. Sorry! I was only thankful it wasn't the young girl."

Owen drove. The car breached the brow of Greenhow Hill at speed. The tight, wooded roadsides suddenly vanished in a blur as the moorland swiftly opened to either side and the quality of the dying evening light flooded the car. Owen dropped the sun visor immediately. The further they drove, the greater the spread of the evening sky filled their view; the main colour seemed incongruous, rich, almost turquoise. Occasionally, owing to the undulation of the road, the sun streamed horizontally directly at the windscreen and Cyril slipped a pair of aviator sunglasses onto his nose.

"How the bloody hell do you see, Owen?"

"I partly close my eyes." It was said in all seriousness. A small grin had appeared on his lips.

Cyril gripped the side of his seat as he glanced at Owen. It was no lie.

As they approached their destination, New Road, a spur leading from the A6265, blue strobe lights were visible. The road seemed barred by a stationary police estate car parked diagonally, the source of the flashing strobes. Owen turned onto New Road, the police estate edging forward as the officer responded to the corresponding lights flashing within the approaching car's grille and upper windscreen. Owen slowed to a stop, two wheels on the grass verge. The officer smiled and nodded in greeting.

"Layby down on the left. Doctor and the CSI team is already there."

Cyril removed his sunglasses. The road, a single track, was bordered on both sides by a grass verge and dry-stone wall. They continued slowly. The rear of a police van displayed diagonal striped orange and yellow chevrons. It was clear to see as they approached. So too was the police tape stretched across the road demarcating the area of the crime scene. A white suited figure moved within the area; a police officer stood outside the flimsy barrier, his attention drawn by the approaching vehicle. A blue and white forensic tent was visible, erected well away from the left-hand wall on the moorland some distance from the road. The smaller of the two gates set within the wall, the one used for the footpath, was being assessed by one of the CSI.

Cyril and Owen grabbed fluorescent jackets from the

boot before making their way to the blue and white tape. To the right was another car which Cyril presumed to be that of the Forensic Pathologist. He did not recognise the vehicle and much further down the road was positioned an ambulance, semi-silhouetted against the contrasting sunset sky. On closer inspection, he observed a number of people milling around the ambulance. Cyril paused and counted seven.

The CSM walked to meet them. "DCI Bennett. Inspector Owen? I thought it would take you longer."

Cyril looked at Owen. "I take a couple of Kwells when I receive calls of this nature as Mr Lewis Hamilton here has lost none of his desire to arrive at his destination before he leaves the station carpark. I've needed to lie down after many a quick journey."

It brought a smile to the officer's face. "I get sick on boats and buses and I can't read in a car. I understand fully, it's debilitating. My husband's a keen sailor and so he sails alone!"

Cyril pointed to the tent set a few hundred metres from the gates that broke the wall in two places. A CSI approached it whilst deliberately moving well off the footpath.

"The Pathologist is in there now. As SIO will you be wishing to view the victim?"

"I'll wait, thanks. The path?" He pointed to the wooden signpost.

"The footpath leads to Skyreholme, Firbeck but also to Parcevall Hall. The layby's been left clear as they'll be searching for evidence of any vehicle that might have been used. The footpath's been closed at the lower end. Looking at the victim's clothing or should I say lack of it, I can assume he wasn't hiking."

She handed Cyril an iPad. "Preliminary images taken by CSI." Most used mobile phones without the SIM cards owing to their quality and flexibility. "The body's face down and was discovered just off the footpath in relatively long grass by a walking group at about 19.30. They rang for an ambulance and the police. They're down with the medics who I believe have given them the once over. Finding a body in broad daylight is something you don't expect, especially here. They were going to try resuscitation. One of the group is a retired nurse but she soon realised the victim was dead. Each has agreed to give a sample for profiling against DNA transfer. Strangely, one mentioned there was a strong scent on or near the body but couldn't describe it. Like a perfume. The officer first at the scene questioned them but there's only so much they can say. Their names and contact details are on file." She pointed to the iPad. "I believe they saw a couple of cars pass the gate as they were walking from the valley but neither stopped. We're checking for any CCTV coverage. Here the cameras are attached to farm buildings but as you can imagine they are few and far between. We're not optimistic. One other walker passed the group down near Parcevall Hall so there's an assumption the body arrived here after he passed through this spot, or there's even a possibility he just didn't see it. The group passed him about forty-five minutes before discovering the body so he was well down into the valley."

Owen leaned over Cyril's shoulder. The man in the photographs was face down as they had been informed.

Cyril was amazed to see he was dressed in what looked like a T-shirt and jeans. He was shod in almost perfect white training shoes. “Thought you said he wasn’t dressed?” Cyril looked at the CSM.

“No, I remarked that he wasn’t dressed appropriately for walking in the area.”

“Do we have an approximate age?” Cyril asked as he checked his phone for Google maps, occasionally looking back at the officer in anticipation. He located his present position before allowing his stare to follow the footpath. The glow from the phone’s screen faintly illuminated his face as the evening was drawing in.

“He’s fairly young, in his twenties.”

Cyril turned to Owen and frowned.

“We’ll know more when the doctor’s finished.” She tipped her head towards the position of the now concealed body.

“We put a drone up on arrival to check the general vicinity for walkers. There’s a gully way down there, Troller’s Gill, and people walk through there but they’d be invisible to spot from this location. The footage is there for you to inspect but there was no one on the footpath nor, from what we could see, in the gully. Heat sensitive imagery was also used but only sheep were identified. As you’re aware, the drone saves trampling the crime scene and the surrounds.”

Cyril wanted to say something about the bleeding obvious but resisted as he inspected the satellite image on his phone and located the gully.

“Troller’s Gill, Owen. Means, I believe, the Troll’s arse, the crack breaking the land. Quaint Yorkshire term. From my secular knowledge, Owen, it was the home of the

Barghest …" He didn't finish but paused and looked across at the sudden movement by the forensic tent.

The Forensic Pathologist walked back along the designated, controlled pathway marked in accordance with the CSM instruction. He was fully covered in PPE, a hooded oversuit, mask and overshoes. Even the case he carried seemed to be protected. He paused by the wall and began removing the designated clothing before stuffing it into a clinical waste bin positioned by the wall. His second pair of gloves was the penultimate clothing discarded, the last being his face mask. He stretched before slipping through the larger gate, keeping to the step plates and approached the crime scene boundary tape. Cyril and Owen moved forward as he introduced himself. His face and name were familiar to Cyril as Julie had mentioned he had been temporarily appointed to the north east team. Dr White put down his bag, removed his handkerchief before wiping his face. He blew his nose loudly.

His first words were directed at the CSM. "Dead, possibly before he arrived here. He's been dead six or seven hours." His words slipped away as he blew his nose again. "There was a strong smell of perfume on the body which is most unusual, not a masculine smell, probably to mask something else. I've asked for the head and hands to be bagged as well as the shoes being removed for further assessment. The head … particularly the mouth." He paused and shook his head. "Most peculiar and may have been the cause of death but let's not jump to conclusions. As I say, most peculiar."

Cyril approached. "DCI Bennett, SIO and this is Inspector Owen. You must be Dr Peter White."

White paused obviously at a disadvantage.

"My wife is Dr Julie Pritchett, she still uses her maiden name professionally. She mentioned you'd strayed north if only on a temporary basis."

"Temporarily blown off course shall we say. Cyril, I believe?" He smiled and returned his handkerchief to his pocket.

"Correct."

"She's made me most welcome and often mentions you. I had hoped we might meet in better circumstances but then this is what we do!"

"Could you suggest an approximate age of the victim?" Cyril was eager to ascertain if the body was possibly that of Kadare.

"No more than thirty. If we could cut them open and count the rings it would be a lot more easy." His words seemed callous but when dealing with death on a daily basis Cyril could understand.

"I'd say Mediterranean or Eastern European. Asphyxiation." The word ran on as if he were contemplating the science. "I don't detect there was any kind of struggle so he was probably rendered unconscious. I believe I can say one thing for certain, Detective Inspector, if he did walk through that gate then he didn't walk alone. As you know, if carried or dragged in some way, the forensics people should soon discover corroborative evidence." He turned towards the CSM and smiled. "It's in your capable hands."

The CSM nodded.

The doctor picked up his bag. "Will you be joining me for the autopsy, Detective Chief Inspector?"

Cyril shook his head. "Owen, here. He'll be with you,

has a penchant for them where as I ..."

The doctor pulled a face, a look that could be misinterpreted as a smile of disappointment and moved towards his car.

Cyril handed the iPad back to the CSM and thanked her. "You're wise regarding the sailing, unfortunately I have little choice other than to walk!" He winked at her.

According to the doctor, the crime scene was in safe hands and Cyril had neither doubt about her management nor any need to view the body. Owen on the other hand quickly donned PPE and made his way across to the tent escorted by one of the CSI.

Cyril stood and leaned on the side of the car. *Two essentially disparate men, both accused of trying to meet underaged girls are now missing after being allegedly exposed as paedophiles by the same group*. He broke off his train of thought momentarily and looked across towards the forensic tent. *One, at least, we've found.*

To add to his concern their faces were on the police social media platforms as well as on the local news and yet, to his knowledge, there had been no sightings or reports detailing their present whereabouts. He stared across the open landscape. Down in the valley the pallid evening light had succumbed to a covering, a black blanket of heavy mist had crept in whilst the sky to the west was streaked and smudged with the remnants of the sunset's rich colours. Cyril paused and took a moment to appreciate the view as Owen approached. "It's a beautiful thing nature, Owen, but it can be a bloody cruel world."

"It's Kadare. You know what?"

Cyril turned.

"White's probably spot on. His trainers are so clean. They were bagging them. The laces were undone, just stuffed in by the tongue. He didn't walk there unless he was on tiptoes. There's a funny appearance to his mouth and nose."

Neither spoke until they were back in the car.

As if on a completely different tack Owen spoke as he manoeuvred the car in what he hoped would be a three-point turn. "Just relieved it wasn't the girl." He paused. "Latest news, she was supposedly staying at a girlfriend's overnight but from all accounts that was only partially true. They'd arranged to meet later in the afternoon, early evening depending on your interpretation of time. Not directly after school as this friend works but we need to confirm that. If they didn't meet until later, whom did she meet and why? Even if she did meet this older friend, there's still a stretch of time when her parents would be unaware of what she was doing or even that she'd gone missing. What I'm getting at is if we imagine there's no friend as such and let's say the parents didn't keep a tight rein on her, after all she's sixteen ..." He could see the thought process etched on Cyril's face. "They just wanted to meet people they might be denied seeing. It's happened in a few cases where kids go missing even those who have protective parents. Where there's a will there's a way."

Cyril nodded. "Forbidden fruit. On some occasions they end up like that poor sod we've just seen."

"Didn't you go places when you were a nipper where you weren't supposed to go and made up stories to cover your tracks?"

"I did, Owen, but they were different times."

The rest of the journey home was in complete contrast to the outward trip – it was slow and sedate. The whole mixed-up set of facts tumbled round in Cyril's head as he attempted to make some sort of sense that was both real and logical. He watched the hedgerows grow slowly darker and the headlights flood the road way into the distance.

Chapter 11

Cyril looked at the cup resting on the saucer. A faint wisp of steam rose bringing with it the smell of the tea. He would love to sit back with an electronic cigarette, drink the tea and let the world drift by. His eyes fell on the grey filing cabinet opposite and his thoughts turned to the photograph trapped within. He breathed a sigh.

"Each one, each person is as important as the other." The words were almost a whisper, reverent and genuine. The light in the room dimmed as someone stood in the doorway. It was Brian Smirthwaite. His breathing was heavy as he stopped.

"Just heard. The search you requested. We've found clothing. We think it's the girl's."

"Where?" Cyril stood.

"Hornbeam Square West, a road on the industrial estate not too far from where Kadare was intercepted. It was in a plastic shopping bag and only her school stuff, there was no underwear or shoes. Her clothes were all neatly folded too. They were inside a salt bin, those roadside yellow containers. There's a few in that area. Not used a lot at this time of year. A dog's nose found them."

"She's done a runner and was planning on coming back for them. As you say, who'd look inside those now? Maybe she had a change of clothes, wanted to appear older, more mature if she were meeting someone. Bit of a Cinderella. There were plenty of places she could have changed clothing along that route without being seen. Mobile phone?"

"Checking and also investigating CCTV and ANPR for cars arriving and leaving the area. There are no cameras on that specific road as far as we know but plenty on the industrial estate. The clothes have gone to Forensics. Shakti and Family Liaison are at the Thomas's house."

"As much info and as soon as. Thanks, Brian."

***

Owen checked the clock on the wall. The doctor had just started the autopsy as he arrived. The victim's body was naked and a technician was finalising the fingernail clip. His clothing had gone for forensic examination. Dr Peter White looked up at Owen through the Perspex visor, the mask beneath muffling the welcome.

"I hear DCI Bennett is not one for this part of the job." There was a slight hint of disdain trapped within his words.

"He never has liked seeing or smelling body fluids, particularly his own. I suppose it wouldn't be good for us all to be alike," Owen shot back defensively.

There was a pause as if a safe distance was being marked between them.

"I wasn't insinuating a weakness just ..." He looked down at the body and then back. "We may have been wrong about his time of death but I'll have a greater understanding of that soon. Although the body was blanchable at the scene, it does not preclude his being brought there after death, maybe prostrate in the back of a van, but right at this minute I need more evidence. The fact I detected blanching was noted in my findings at the time. You'll know, DI Owen, that blanching is possible for eight to twelve hours after death. We can also say for certain he didn't die of hypothermia as such circumstances would lead to a distinguishing discolouration of livor mortis and I saw none. It is what was in the mouth and nasal passages that is also of interest. Now whether that's pre or post death is what we must discover."

"And rigor mortis?" Owen asked the question to emphasise the fact that he had been in this very spot before on more than one occasion.

Dr White paused resting his gloved hands on the side of the stainless-steel table. "It was noticeable at the time too so my prediction was accurate to be around three to four hours. You will know that lower temperatures speed up the onset of rigor mortis but as you attended the crime scene, you'll know the day had been fine and the evening relatively warm so that may have slowed the process marginally."

"So, Dr White, your prediction of time of death?"

"From the temperature taken at the scene to the evidence before me, I'd predict five hours prior to discovery but we're not here to predict, we're here to determine the facts. That's my role in life."

***

Shakti sat opposite Gina's parents. There had been a good deal of upset but Gina's mother had been able to identify the items of clothing from the photographs that were spread across the coffee table like morbid Tarot cards.

"She's always been known as Gina May, my Gina May, I always said. She's a good girl. Works hard at school, she's never found it easy."

"Did she often stay over with friends?"

There was a nod of the head but then a pause. "Since she left Primary School. She went to friends and friends came here. I liked it when they were here, I knew what they were up to. They can be so vulnerable to peer pressure." She paused and wiped a tear from her cheek as she shuffled the photographs on the table. "You have to trust your kids. Do you have children?" Mrs Thomas looked at both Shakti and Maxine Geary, the Family Liaison Officer.

"Two, both grown." Maxine smiled. "I understand just what you're saying. Mothers can never rest, we've been there, we know ..."

Mrs Thomas tried to smile but failed.

"None." Shakti's answer was quick. "I also don't want children and that's by choice. My career comes first I'm afraid." She quickly changed tack. "With whom did she say she was staying?" She did not mention the information they had received about an older friend.

"Her friend Paula but that wasn't true. I called her mum as soon as the school had let me know she was absent."

"Has she been acting differently recently?" Maxine leaned forward. "My girls certainly changed on more than one occasion, sometimes they became quite reclusive, insular. It was often like treading on egg shells when I asked certain questions." The comment was sensitively put.

Mrs Thomas wiped another tear and a chuckle came, it was involuntary and real. "Yes, I've ..." She turned to her husband and slipped her hand on his. "We've been there, particularly when she was a little younger. We've had the sulks and the slamming doors, the total attachment to social media, the 'you don't understand me' but she seemed to grow out of that. She was only happy when buying the latest fashions but that soon waned too. She's the oldest in her year group. People underestimate the consequences of that."

"Her mobile?" Shakti knew the answer but asked anyway.

"Went to answerphone and it's now off. Why would she do that? She goes nowhere without it."

Maxine looked at Shakti. "There could be many reasons. I once dropped mine down the loo. Left it in the back pocket of my jeans."

"Battery life. Because it's turned off does not have a –" Shakti wanted to say *sinister* but stopped herself. "It could be just that. I can assure you both that we are doing what we can to find her."

"Does she have any older girl friends, people who have left school?" Maxine's question brought an immediate response.

***

Cyril studied the two statements taken from pupils who had last seen Gina May. To them she had seemed excited and yet quite anxious as the end of the school day approached.

However, according to both girls she had mentioned she was meeting a friend and staying over, an older girl friend, who was taking her into town, a 'girls' night' they had assumed. According to one, Gina May had money with her. Cyril continued to read. She had left school dressed in her uniform carrying only her school bag. There had been no report of a bag deposited with the clothes in the grit bin.

Cyril read it through a few times. He could understand that Gina May might have a friend of eighteen, a friend who would take her out, allow her to sleep over and then get her back to school but why hide your clothes in a grit bin? It would be far easier to change at the friend's place. *Where were the clothes she would change in to? Had they been placed there in the morning or stashed somewhere else? What secret was she hiding? Who was she deceiving, apart from herself?* He shuffled the papers into an orderly pile as Owen came to the door interrupting his thought process.

"Dr White? Not too sure. Seems to have a worse attitude than Kaner and I never believed that could ever be possible. To be honest, he'd make a bloody good corpse himself and he certainly has the personality to match!"

Cyril raised his eyebrows and pointed to the chair. "Not kind, Owen, not kind but I can certainly understand your opinion from the limited time we spoke at the crime scene."

"What does Julie think?" Owen leaned forward hoping for some gossip.

"Careless talk costs lives, Owen. What news from the spirit world?"

"Our man died, but then we knew that, died from asphyxia but in a curious way. It is believed that he was rendered unconscious at the scene so he did walk through the gate. Contusion to the upper right temple but ..." His finger moved to the area. "Here's the bizarre part, his mouth was then filled with polyurethane expandable foam. Filled the throat and made its way into the nasal cavities." He paused giving Cyril time to fully comprehend what he had just said. It brought the same incredulity to his face as he himself had exhibited when White had given him the details. "As I said bizarre."

"Expandable foam? Builders' foam that's in every DIY shop in the UK?"

"In one, sir. According to White, there has over the last few years been a rise in the number of attempts at suicide using this method but very few have been successful."

"I didn't think it would stick to moist surroundings."

"It is believed the tube was inserted far into the throat and the mouth and nose closed. The foam had only one place to go. As he was unconscious there was no resistance. Hands and nails show there was no defence."

"You had a 'but' when mentioning the temple." Cyril moved his hand to his own as Owen had unconsciously done.

"Right, injury and the resulting bruising according to Dr White, can be difficult to assess. There was no breaking of the skin even though it is tight and close to bone. As you know haematoma takes some time to appear but they can appear even after death." After a short search, Owen removed a scrap of paper from his pocket. He read it out almost in a monotone. "'In many instances, where there is congestion of the cadaver, sufficient blood escape from vessels damaged after death can be indistinguishable from injuries occurring shortly before.' He was suggesting Asadi

Kadare fell to that side after being struck so there's a possible masking of the initial trauma. Further investigation will be carried out, I was informed." Owen placed the scrap of paper onto Cyril's desk.

"Trainers, Owen."

"Here again it's believed they were just slipped on post death, his original shoes were removed. The trainers he was wearing were not tied. The laces were simply stuffed down into the shoes' tongues. At least they were on the correct feet!"

"Thanks, Owen. I take it all of this has been added to the system?"

Owen nodded. "Anything on the other missing folk?"

Cyril frowned and pushed the reports he had been reading across his desk.

Chapter 12

The deep purr from the cat seemed to fill the kitchen with a degree of peace and an acute sense of security. As if vying for full attention, the cat tucked his head and rolled onto his back on the mat, a tactic that had worked before. His deep tortoiseshell colours suddenly gave way to a beige, softer underbelly of straggly fur as he rolled; the tail swished backwards and forwards as if caressing the surrounding air enticingly.

"You're a tart, Tommy, a fickle feline and you bloody well know it!"

Tommy moved towards the outside door and paced from one side to the other asking to be let out.

"Your command is my wish!" The words were but a whisper said with both sincerity and annoyance. "A dog, I feel, would have greater respect for the hand that feeds."

Moving across to the outside door it was opened and the cat slipped through the narrowest of gaps.

The kitchen could best be described as run down but it was habitable. It was equipped with a twin ring camping stove and a toaster. An avocado green kitchenette seemed to lean against one wall as if ducking beneath the many painted beams that ran across the ceiling. The layers of paint were flaky and web-covered and the Belfast sink seemed scarred from a million pots and pans over a long lifetime. The table and chairs were the centrepiece on which the polystyrene box sat; it was clearly the newest object there. The box contents were known. It would be the last delivery. The placement of the first two items had received the desired effect – the request to the public for help with dash cam footage as well as the immediate police interest in the deposited items had been proof enough.

Moving over to the table and lifting the lid revealed another hand. Touching it brought the same degree of revulsion that came when handling the other objects, whether that be the disturbance and unsettling of memories, of secrets, or purely from its unusual texture. The flexible plasticity appeared to shake as if in fear and could not be determined but, at this moment, it seemed unimportant. Although the objects looked so real, the texture certainly could not be described as human but the size and the detail seemed to the eye to be so real. The lines within the palm and at the digital joints were clear enough to be counted, the knuckles proud. Turning it, holding it to the light, the fingernails appeared finely manicured but they were the same colour as the flesh and the least realistic element of the work.

"The last one, the final temptation. 'Idle hands are the devil's plaything.' The writing is there for them to see if they continue to look." The synthetic hand went back into the box.

***

"We've been informed your daughter was planning to meet someone for a night out in town, someone older, we believe female ..." Shakti left the sentence open considering the looks on the faces of Gina May's parents who sat before her, both still trying to come to terms with the situation. "We believe that the sleepover was a deception on this occasion. The question is, Mr and Mrs Thomas, is this the only time she's deceived you or has it happened before, the only difference now being that she failed to go into school? We've checked the local hospitals and I'm relieved to say she has neither been to A&E nor been admitted. Does she have older friends of whom you're aware?"

Mrs Thomas looked at her husband, her confusion was clear but there was something else. Shakti sensed it immediately.

"What is it? Whatever you're thinking please tell us."

"She has a couple of friends whom she met in school, she's known them a while, nice girls. They left a couple of years ago. She told me they'd moved on and she didn't see them now but who knows if she's still friends on social media or if they still see each other? There may be more too but if I push for information, I know she'd clam up, and things would become uncomfortable. Kids push back and that's the last thing I'd want to do, put a rift between us. She was bad enough when she was twelve but then seemed to mature. I want to trust her and I need her to be able to talk to me about anything. I thought she did, I thought we had a good relationship but ..."

"Do you have any names?"

She glanced again at her husband who nodded.

"Elizabeth Green, Gina May called her Liz and the other was Sharon Potts. The school will have their addresses. I don't know them. I met Liz once; she came here one weekend, it could probably have been a couple of years ago, just before she left school. Nice girl. She was excited about starting work. I remember we chatted a lot. She seemed so juvenile in a way and looked up to Gina."

"What work was that?" Maxine asked.

"Shop work. That's as much as I can say."

"Do you have any of Gina May's IT equipment in the house?"

***

Stuart Park took a moment to take in his surroundings. The university was larger than he had imagined and certainly more scenic. The roadway into the campus clearly announced he had arrived at the correct place. He parked where instructed in the email he had received.

Stepping from the car he was impressed by the contrasting architectural style of the numerous building that wrapped the man-made waterway as it tumbled down weirs before settling in a broad, dark mirror-like expanse. Ducks nestled in batches along the concrete banks. He paused to admire the reflections. There was an unnatural calm for such a busy campus.

He glanced at the map he had been sent, took one more look at his surroundings before orientating the map and heading for the designated building.

Within fifteen minutes he had received a warm welcome, a coffee, a brochure detailing the university and a promise that Dr Callum Shaw would be with him in about ten minutes. He checked his watch. He was impressed.

Dr Shaw, once the personal tutor to Gülen Köse, was punctual. He moved quickly along the corridor towards Park, his hand outstretched whilst he glanced at his watch.

"Sorry if I'm a little late. It appears as if you've been well looked after." He tapped the brochure. "I could certainly recommend the Creative Arts programme this university has to offer." He smiled. "Come, you don't have all day, DC Park."

The room they arrived at was comfortable yet unusual as two walls were constructed of glass. "The 'goldfish bowls' I call these. I like to believe they were designed for their aesthetic qualities of light and space but maybe you might see another more politically correct reason, maybe for the exposure. Do you wish to have a degree more privacy?"

"I'd feel more comfortable."

Shaw leaned towards one of the walls and touched a button set within a stainless steel plate. Immediately the transparent glass became a misty-grey opaque. "The wonders of modern science, DC Park. To think we used to have curtains and blinds! How very twentieth century." He laughed and settled into the chair. "How may I help? You mentioned Gülen had gone missing, I was disturbed to hear this but you're aware I left ..."

Park held up a hand and stopped Shaw mid-sentence. "You ceased being her tutor during her final year, the early part. Just tell me your thoughts on the young woman." He placed a Dictaphone on the desk. "Is this alright?"

Dr Shaw smiled, nodded and leaned back in the chair

before steepling his fingers. "Let's see. Hard working, particularly skilful, not only within her draughtsmanship but she had a keen eye for perspective and scale. She not only worked well in both her two dimensional tasks but also in three dimensional. She was dedicated and a perfectionist. You could say she was driven to succeed. On the whole, overseas students seem to have a greater determination, a deliberate focus. Maybe that's to do with the costs, it's bloody expensive for them to study here. They have an understanding too of a responsibility to the family unit and the sacrifices they may have had to endure to fund their studies. I think we have lost that here in the UK."

The words 'three dimensional' struck a chord. "Sculpture?"

"Very much so. She worked well in clay. She was experimental which always excites. She even produced some pieces working in things like car body filler – the metal filler for repairing dents and she also worked with soapstone, carving directly from the block. She was certainly imaginative when it came to her choice of materials." He let his hands drop palm down on the table and a smile demonstrated a change of thought. "I don't know if this is relevant but it showed the degree of imagination that moves some to be so different from the rest of the group. I had one student who took moulds of a number of lads' erect penises before creating a wall sculpture comprising about twenty-five! Could you believe twenty-five guys would agree to work with her? Now that was certainly outside the box and the most bizarre in my teaching experience if not a little weird. Certain individuals did frown on seeing it and I don't think it would have made the end of year show."

"Really? Was that allowed?" Park's tone reflected his incredulity.

"Why ever not! The course includes life study, DC Park, the drawing and painting of a variety of naked folk, young and old, so why not? It's not as if she made door handles or coat hooks from them. It was an interesting study. I was amazed how many people who saw the final piece took a while to see what they were actually looking at. If anything, if I were to be honest, it resembled a large sea anemone. Something created out of context and vividly coloured can camouflage most things."

Park took a moment to compose himself. "Relationships? I believe she had a boyfriend and I also believe she had a perfect attendance record."

"Boyfriend, yes. Give me a minute. Coulson?" He looked at Park but the officer remained silent. "Nice lad, a little older that the rest if my memory serves me well. He too was a hard worker and also very talented. I think he was her guiding light technically. He contacted me about a month after I left. He said he was concerned for her, believed she was losing her direction. All I can say is what I know. I can't speak for the present but only the relationship, the professional relationship, we had. He only called me the once. I did ask him to contact me again if his concerns remained the same. I assumed as I didn't hear that she'd got back on track."

"She never returned home during her time at university. Were you aware of that?" Park leaned forward. It was something that had intrigued him.

"Some students move abroad because their choice of

university is the most appropriate for both them and their chosen subject. Others just want to get life experiences and use the languages they have learned. And there are some who want all of those things but they also want freedom, freedom from a country, parents or siblings, maybe a break from that claustrophobic family unit of which we spoke earlier. They want a fresh start, they want to be on their own, stand on their own feet. That might be to prove to themselves or to prove to others they are independent people in their own right. However, I felt there was something more. She never liked to talk about family. I believe her father moved to work abroad when she came to Leeds. I never saw photographs of her family, that I felt was quite unusual."

"And Köse. What was her reason for being here?"

"The million-dollar question. The best course to suit her particular skill set and talent. Her reason? I don't know. What I do know is that whilst I was there, whilst I was her personal tutor, she was dedicated, professional, functional. Her attendance was exemplary and importantly we got on well. She demonstrated no real insecurities either personally or within her studies. If it's relevant there were a number of foreign students who remained in the UK without venturing home. They often took the opportunity to travel both here and in Europe."

"Did you ever meet her outside of the university setting, Dr Shaw?" Park observed Shaw's body language as he landed the question. There was little physical response.

"Indeed. On more than one occasion."

Park stared directly at Shaw.

"You want to know more even though I don't need to

expand?" He paused returning the eye contact. "I, like a doctor, have students' confidentiality to consider but owing to the gravity of the situation that goes by the board. We extended our discussions over meals. I took her to both public and private galleries to develop more fully her understanding of the subject. You have to remember that in my position certain students remind me of myself at their stage of creative understanding and development. I too had mentors, one in particular, she was female but our relationship was always professional. The ability to hone their developing skill and understanding, guide them further along their chosen career path is not only a challenge but an absolute privilege – you might say a pleasure. She's not the first student I've given my time to outside the normal hours if there's ever such a time scale. I'll continue to share my knowledge, passion, skill and even if I do say so myself, my generous spirit."

"Can you give me the names of two other students from the same cohort to whom you've demonstrated your generosity of spirit?"

Callum Shaw's demeanour immediately changed. "There's a cruel insinuation within your tone, DC Park, that I neither like nor will I tolerate. Just what are you suggesting, that I groomed Gülen to get her into bed? I find your intimation deplorable."

Park wanted to respond with the word 'touché' but thought better, in order to let that and any unintended insinuation drop. It would get him nowhere and he needed the man's full co-operation. "It could be suggested that your leaving might have had a direct result on the young woman, a change that not only affected her work but that of her personal life."

"I've no control over that if it be true but I do feel saddened if that's the case. I thought she was stronger."

Park took out an electronic tablet and passed it across. "Did you know that this is an example of the type of work she submitted for her final show?"

Shaw's eyebrows lifted and he flicked through the images. "They have some technical merit but that's all I can say. This does not reflect the girl's abilities. Give me five minutes."

He stood and exited the room leaving the tablet on the table. He returned with a laptop. Within moments he had found images of Gülen's work. "Here, compare and contrast."

Park studied the images. The quality of the draughtsmanship was outstanding. He stopped at one, a sculpture of a pair of hands. They brought a tingle to his neck as he thought of the hand found at the building on Otley Road. "This?" Park pointed to the hands.

"It was so impressive and it wasn't all she produced. You have an eye for quality if I may say so. She was fascinated by a sculptor by the name of Lorenzo Quinn, Italian, do you know of him?" Seeing Park shake his head he continued. "Concentrates on the human form, particularly hands. He plays with scale and if you research his monumental works, some are set in Venice, you'll understand the attraction. I also think he demonstrates the power and yet in other ways the fragility of the human form – hands can one minute caress and within a second, strike, all by their change of shape. Although a contemporary artist he is inspired by the works of Michelangelo and Rodin and that should be clear for you to see." Shaw took the laptop and *Googled* the artist. "Here, you can clearly see how he was influenced and therefore how she might have been fascinated by his skill. The hands, according to Quinn, are in his opinion the most challenging part of the human body to recreate."

Park looked at the variety of images presented.

"Tell me, Dr Shaw, were the hands produced by Gülen taken from a mould?"

Shaw frowned at the näivety of the question. "Yes, but the initial clay modelling was her own work. She didn't put plaster round someone's hand if that's what you're suggesting. As I said, she was very talented. So, to see this later work," he tapped Park's electronic tablet, "I must say I'm surprised if not a little disappointed."

Park sat back. "Thank you very much for your time. It's been of great interest. All we have to do now is try to find this missing young woman." He stood and proffered a hand.

"I'm sorry I can't help any further. I'd be grateful if you could let me know as soon as she's found."

Park nodded. "One last thing. Did you communicate or meet with her after you left to relocate here?"

There was a pause. Park studied Shaw's features again carefully.

"As it happens, yes. She called me a couple of times and we met once. I had an appointment in Leeds and we had lunch."

Park sat back down.

Chapter 13

Cyril flicked through the auction house catalogue pausing at a bronze figure, Lot 17. He read the description before glancing at the sculpture that sat to the right of his computer keyboard. It was the rough and yet delicate maquette bought by the team as a wedding present. Picking it up he weighed it in his hand whilst studying the details. His thoughts turned to the rubberised head and hand believed to be moulded from Jones. *What secrets are trapped within the mouldings that we cannot see?*

There was a knock as Park tapped the door's architrave. The interruption immediately flushed the thought from his mind.

"A minute, sir?" Stuart Park spoke with a certain eagerness.

Cyril replaced the small statue and stood showing a degree of enthusiasm as Park entered. "Do you have something?"

"I interviewed Dr Callum Shaw on home ground." He held up the Dictaphone. "Gülen Köse was fascinated by an artist by the name of Lorenzo Quinn, a man who seemed to specialise in the sculpting of hands, bloody big ones too on occasion."

"I'm familiar with his work." Cyril sat as Park pulled out a chair.

"Although we've seen the later work she produced, the stuff that seemed to disappoint a number of people, I've seen some of her other stuff. She's good, not that I'm an authority but I know what I like and ... anyway, she did some interesting work on hands. They were bronze or maybe he said resin but the accuracy was truly amazing. He seemed genuinely shocked when I showed him the work she presented in her final show."

Cyril tapped the keyboard and the images of the face and hand they had found appeared. He enlarged the image and contemplated the detail.

"Even if you sculpt the clay, you still take a mould and then ... positive to negative and back to positive if I followed the process he discussed." Park tried to remember what Shaw had said.

"Owen suggested in the first instance that rather than taking a mould from the real person it was sculpted. That would be determined by the accuracy of scale, it would have to match perfectly if taken from ..." Cyril paused. "That, Stuart, can only be judged by a direct comparison and owing to his absence that cannot be done. The fingers on that hand found held no true prints but impressions and according to Forensics they didn't match those we hold of the girl or Jones. They apparently are not a match for anyone involved to date."

"In my opinion Shaw could well have been having an affair with the student. He was very defensive and yet admitted to seeing her outside of the university and, importantly, even after he left. He was of the belief that she didn't return home owing to some domestic issues. She never divulged what those might have been. I immediately thought that it might well have been some kind of abuse and maybe either physical or sexual. Her father went to work abroad on her leaving. Maybe that's just me. I've checked but so far, we have nothing back from the Turkish police to say any of the family were known to them."

"Very speculative but what's your gut feeling about any possible unprofessional misconduct by Shaw?"

"At first I believed there might have been a possibility but ..." Park shook his head.

"So, he became a father figure, a confidant and mentor. That's why she never missed a personal session, why he inspired her work and maybe why she fell off the edge of the cliff when he left. Maybe there was an attraction on her side, a father substitute but then she learned Shaw was the consummate professional. So, I ask again, in your opinion, how close were they, Stuart?"

Park exhaled audibly. "He was extremely plausible, seemed to care about the girl but maybe more about her work. He showed genuine concern when he saw her later work. You might say he was shocked and disappointed as a parent might be."

"I trust your instinct but I want a full background check on Shaw. I want to write him off, maybe I want to trust him and his judgement. I also need to know how these bloody things were made." He tapped the computer screen. "Check the university for an expert."

"Shaw mentioned that Leeds was linked in 2019 to a sculpture festival, it was run over a hundred days and was in partnership with world renowned artists and researchers. The university supported the event, the idea being to re-establish the importance of sculpture in the area."

"Maybe she was involved, the timescale puts her at the beginning of her university course. Contact the Yorkshire Sculpture Park and find an expert, also contact The Hepworth. I'd like a definitive on this very puzzle."

***

Cyril Bennett entered the Incident Room and looked at the whiteboards. He thrust his hands in his pockets and stared at the photograph taken of the two objects. The room was busy. There was a low hum made up of mumbling voices and computer fans. April approached.

"We have a sighting from a member of the public of what we hope is Gina May." Her voice did not hide her excitement.

Cyril turned. "Where?"

"Ripon, well not exactly but she was seen on the number 36, Harrogate to Ripon bus. We're checking for CCTV from the bus as well as at both bus stations."

Cyril hardly gave her time to finish. "Was she alone?" he asked even though he knew his presumption would not be valid.

"Interestingly, she was with a man."

A look of surprise swept across his face. April predicted the next question and she was correct.

"An illicit boyfriend?"

***

Cyril had checked for further information from Forensics not only on Kadare's death but also the fake body parts. There was nothing forthcoming other than what Owen had reported after the autopsy. Toxicology and samples from both Kadare's body and clothing would take longer. He turned, propped himself against a table and looked at the large screen positioned at the far end of the Incident Room. They were about to play a preview of the planned televised appeal made by Gina May's parents before the sighting. However, the Police Search Advisor had advised it still be aired locally. Not knowing with whom she had travelled the risk assessment still placed her in possible harm's way.

In his career, Cyril had seen many such appeals. It was heartbreaking to see the raw emotions wrought from frightened parents. However, these pleas often led to direct responses from the public and although traumatic to watch, he felt as SIO it had to be transmitted.

The response he had received from the Turkish police after they had interviewed Gülen's mother had been woeful. As they already knew, the father had been working in Germany and had implied that he had disowned her. She had abandoned the family after all the sacrifices they had made. They had received reports that she had frequented places with men, consumed alcohol and gone against the promises she had made to him on taking up her studies. She had not kept in touch with her mother nor siblings at key times. From all accounts he had washed his hands of her. From reading the report there seemed little concern on his behalf that she was missing and that she had outstayed her visa. It brought an uneasy feeling to his stomach. How could a father turn away from his daughter no matter what they had done, especially a daughter who was miles from home?

***

On opening the rear van door, the polystyrene box had moved along the metal floor before stopping at the protruding wheel arch. Small beads had broken away from the lower corners of the box and had spread, confetti-like across the floor. A quick blow sent them in all directions like worthless flotsam. They soon settled. Lifting the box lid, the single item was transferred to a carrier bag. The metal hook attached to the wrist was tucked in towards the palm to save it protruding from the bag.

Raglan Street was busy and yet parking had been easier than expected. This drop would be the most difficult considering the use of cameras at the target – Harrogate Magistrates' Court. Situated at the lower end of Victoria Avenue and set a short distance from the pavement it was built of stone and blended well with the street's older and more formal appearance. Although it appeared that there were no CCTV cameras on the façade itself, there would be some within the doorway. The sign announcing this to be the Harrogate Justice Centre brought a smile. *Let's hope this final act will bring about that justice and fairness.* This thought caused a pause to the walk as the past was brought to mind. Even on this broad avenue with the sky blue and the sun shining there seemed a chill that induced a shiver to the skin.

Victoria Avenue was unusual in that parking was

allowed along the centre of the road as well as the road edges. Walking confidently, the Justice Centre was ahead and to the left. Reaching into the bag with gloved hands, the object was removed before the hook was adjusted. As the wall and fence to the front of the building started to bend towards the entrance steps, the central handrail became visible as it protruded onto the paved area. This was the target. Looking away from any potential cameras in the doorway, the hand holding the object was stretched to full extent as the hook was slipped over the lower rail and released. It had been critical to keep it away from touching anything for fear of collecting any incriminating forensic evidence. Had they dared to look they would have seen the false hand swing fleetingly with the momentum from the swift action but it soon came to rest. It was now a case of moving back to the van as unobtrusively as possible in the belief the object would be found quickly and acted upon. Whether its significance would be appreciated was in some ways irrelevant.

***

"Just the sighting as reported." April looked crestfallen. "The bloody camera system on the bus was faulty. According to the engineers at the depot, they're not as reliable as they would like. However, their very presence often serves as a deterrent. I've spoken to the witness on the bus, a Mrs Donna Wilbor. She believes the couple weren't on the bus on leaving Harrogate but she remembers they got off on Harrogate Road just before the bridge entering Ripon."

"I know the place." Cyril moved closer. "So, I suppose

nothing from Ripon bus station? What about Harrogate?"

"Nothing for the time that specific number 36 left but there are about nineteen stops along the route. If they're keeping out of sight then they wouldn't use the main stations, they'd use an isolated stop."

"Maybe but they'd be aware the bus has cameras which seems to soften that argument."

"Faulty ones, unfortunately. We're checking for any cameras near the stops along the route into Ripon and also officers and traffic personnel in the area have been alerted. Our social media pages have received an update with their ..."

"Descriptions?" Cyril moved even closer towards April's desk.

She turned her notebook towards him. He read the information before tapping the page. "She's not in trouble, she's in a relationship. Done a runner, she's complicit," he announced. "My experience says she'd nothing to do with Asadi Kadare. Their geographical proximity was just co-incidence." He hit the desk with the palm of his hand. "This is a distraction we could well have done without, April. Put out an urgent request to hotels and known B&B's, cafés and restaurants in that area. It'll just be a matter of time. We have a modern-day Romeo and Juliet, that's my guess."

"In that case do we take it down a level on the risk assessment?"

"No, certainly not. We work on evidence and not on anyone's assumptions, particularly mine!"

"There was something else, another passenger got off the bus just after them. He'd been sitting behind them. According to Wilbor, he seemed to loiter until they headed towards the centre. He then followed. That's not a popular stop at that time of day. Do you want me to contact her and ask a few more questions?"

Cyril paused, before his hand returned to the notepad. "Your judgement, April."

Chapter 14

Owen sat outside The Little Ale House, he had folded the pram and leaned it against the wall. The small front yard contained six tables and an assortment of mismatched wooden chairs. The low sun had filtered through the gap in the opposite buildings and flooded the space bringing with it a degree of warmth. Christopher sat on his father's knee as Owen made the sound of a horse's hooves on stone, bouncing his giggling son whilst holding his hands. Cyril watched as he approached. Considering the missing people for whom they searched it was so good to see a parent enjoying his child. He leaned on the metal railing positioned along the low stone wall.

"It's your Uncle Cyril." Owen spoke with a child-like voice as he leaned Christopher towards the man with the outstretched hand. A smile came to the three of them. He approached and rubbed the child's bonnet-covered head. "Pint, Owen?" Cyril was already turning to go in and order.

"Just a half, driving and also in charge of this monster." He lifted the boy and buried his face into the child's stomach and blew a long raspberry. A loud laugh erupted from the wriggling boy as his legs kicked and the laughter turned to giggles.

Within minutes Cyril was outside and sitting holding Christopher, the giggles and laughter swiftly waned as his arms reached for his father.

"He's an acquired taste my son. You'll get used to him in time." Owen took the child and winked at Cyril. "You either have it or you don't and looking at his face ..."

Cyril picked up his pint. "These never complain."

"When Hannah arrives, we're hoping he'll have settled and we can have an early Italian meal in relative peace but those occasions are few and far between. He's going to be a copper as he's always so inquisitive."

"Like his father, frightened of missing something especially when there's food on offer!"

Owen passed Christopher to Cyril who held him at arm's length as he unfolded the pram and then slid in the wriggling child. "He'll soon go off. I believe there's been another body part found."

"Another hand. Strangely enough it was left outside The Justice Centre." He took a sip of beer. "The more I think about it, the more I'm convinced this is all some bizarre hoax."

Owen picked up his beer. "There's neither rhyme nor reason to someone taking that much trouble. Nothing still on either Jones or the Turkish girl? Ghoul. Bloody strange nickname. There's a link between the two. I read Park's report. She could have made them and she wouldn't have needed him, just some good photographs. I said that and you pooh-poohed it." Owen looked directly at Cyril as he took a huge gulp from his glass.

"Keen as mustard as usual, Owen."

Hannah saved the day as she leaned over the wall. “Afternoon, Cyril. Hope my boy is behaving in this male domain.

Cyril stood. “Which boy? The little one’s been as good as gold. Lovely to see you. You look so well. I believe you’re popping over the road.” He pointed to the Italian restaurant. “I must say, Hannah, you are looking really well. Motherhood really suits you. That young man has brought out the softer side of Owen too.”

“Thank you. I’ve never been happier. Please give my love to Julie.”

“I’ll do that, thank you. Enjoy!”

Owen stood and wheeled the pram and tapped Cyril’s shoulder. “I’ve been informed that briefing is at eight. I believe we also have one of the members of ShadowLink being questioned?”

“With April this afternoon.” Owen guided the pram onto the pavement.

“And Owen, at the briefing, please bring tea in a matching cup and saucer, a reward for your earlier prophetic deduction.” He raised his glass and watched them leave.

***

Anna Murray had been defensive and belligerent since she had been cautioned and informed that the interview would be recorded for all concerned. The group’s solicitor had met with her and sat to her left. Her facial expression gave little away as Murray continued to profess constantly the group’s innocence. She declared they had a right to demonstrate the evil of the paedophiles who searched constantly for young victims on the internet.

"If the police did their jobs people like us wouldn't have to take the law into our own hands. We also don't know who these illegal migrants are. They just shove them in hotels in perfectly respectable areas, allow them to do whatever they want to do at the taxpayers' expense."

April had heard it all before. It was as if her outspoken protestations were recorded and on a loop. She had also made the decision not to get into a discussion about the rights and wrongs of the Government's policy on immigration.

"One man, one of these migrants is dead, the very same man you bullied and frightened. His command of the language was better than many but at best you could only class it as average but still you were determined to frighten him. Does that not make you feel any type of guilt?" April did not give her time to answer. "There could be a link between your interception and his murder. If evidence is found to confirm …"

"The video was only posted to you. It never went live on social media."

The solicitor nodded and tapped the file in front of her as if confirming Murray's statement. She spread her hand on the table as if giving a clue to the direction she should take. It was not missed.

"There are only five of our group and through Crimestoppers the police were witness to the videos so, Detective Inspector Richmond, I strongly refute that." She turned to look at the woman to her left. "Our group does not want to send the lunatic fringe of vigilantes onto those we snare, we just want their activities investigated by yourselves and if you choose to support a policy that continues to put the microscope to your blind eye then so be it. We will, however, continue to pursue them."

"Why did you confront Kadare where you did?"

"That's where he planned to meet our bait. It was his suggestion. You've seen the WhatsApp messages. It's all there for you. Nothing is made up."

"Only the promise of a girl!" April looked at both women before her.

"We had seen him a few days previously. He hung around the outside of the hotel. He was constantly on his phone. Others staying there were in groups but we never once saw him join in. He seemed to be an isolate, a loner. Maybe he was a loner with a history of child abuse. It doesn't sit well in the Albanian community I believe."

"Presumption is never wise when dealing with an issue as serious as this," April responded with a degree of conviction.

The solicitor placed a hand on Murray's arm. There was a pause giving April the opportunity to change direction.

"Similar question then. When you confronted Bernard Jones why did you meet him at the place you did?"

"We received information from someone who lived close by who had seen him on a number of occasions with younger women and girls. We then put out some bait on social media. You've seen the responses he made and you must also have seen the images he posted to her. Bloody disgusting! You've already read what he expected to receive in return. If you follow that through to the logical conclusion, just like Kadare, you know what's going to happen. A life could be ruined or even worse."

"A life was spoiled, let's keep that in mind. It comes down to entrapment." April stressed the word. "You used the words 'bait' and 'snared'. The very reason we do not and will not endorse working with groups like yours."

"But you can't ignore them, the High Court ruled that we do not breach their human rights and many believe that they don't have a right to privacy anyway if they try to commit serious criminal acts to perpetrate the abuse of young children."

April sat back. She knew the High Court ruling after a leading case in Scotland. It still sounded as if the speech were by rote, insincere and without any genuine understanding. "So, in this entrapment, this snaring, did any member of your group send illicit images to Jones to entice him further?"

Anna Murray laughed out loud and allowed her hands to strike the table. "You've seen everything. We're not in the habit of sending lewd images to titillate and encourage these perverted individuals, we just try to bring them to face the consequences of their actions. We send only words, only words and that's enough."

"Fake and false words let's not forget that, words that purport to be from a child." April felt as though she were getting nowhere. "What is your source of the information?"

Murray turned to her solicitor who nodded.

"There was no name but she confirmed she'd been a victim. He'd abused her." Anna Murray sat back. "We didn't get nor did we ask her name but she told us his address and where he would meet his victims. You also note that when we confronted him, he didn't deny it, he just got angry. Two of my group are big lads and that stops any silly aggression. He was relieved when I said it would not be posted on social media and he seemed less concerned when we said the police would be involved. Maybe that tells you something, Inspector, about the public's confidence in your ability to do your job."

"Do you still have her contact details?"

"Sorry, no."

***

The briefing room was busy when Cyril entered. Owen was already seated and the matching cup and saucer sat on the table before an empty seat. The chattering died down as Cyril moved to his place. He checked his watch, shook his wrist and looked again. Owen glanced at his, the watch Cyril had given him to mark the birth of his first child. He was five minutes late and that was unusual.

Cyril opened the proceedings. "Morning. We have progress on two fronts, the first you know about so I don't intend spending too much time talking about it. Gina May has been spotted and we're following that up. We should have answers very soon. You know my thoughts on that and I believe the status shouldn't be downgraded as it's felt by many there's still a potential risk of harm." He looked at his notes and then let his eyes sweep around the room. "Secondly and importantly, the toxicology results for Asadi Kadare have been released. Our dead man was a consumer of a grade A drug and has been using for a while. He had previous too according to this report from the Albanian authorities. It looks as though the interception by the paedophile group might have been the catalyst for his early demise. Word travels quickly and apparently his actions hadn't gone unnoticed within his community even though the information wasn't published. He was seen, he also mentioned it to another migrant from his hotel. Interviews with some of his fellow refugees suggest he was trading drugs. They'd noticed him meeting fellow Albanians away from the hotel. They mentioned flash cars but he never seemed to have money. Two from the hotel also saw his meeting with ShadowLink. That I'm sure would have soon spread.

"Forensics have run tests in the room he shared and class A drug residue has been found. His room companion, also Albanian, is co-operating as we speak. The cruel and unusual circumstances of his death could be linked to the action taken by members of the gangs operating in the Yorkshire area. The way he was killed demonstrates the cruelty and lack of respect for life these gangs show. The strong scent found on the body is another morbid trademark usually left by a group operating in the capital."

"Why did they not just make him disappear long term?" A voice from the back seemed to speak for many.

"Nobody would know, he'd be like a wisp of smoke that would vanish in an instant and his treacherous actions would not be revealed. His death, the reporting of that death nationally, passes down the grapevine of vice. It becomes a life lesson or a warning. Those new conscripts in the many different groups that are spread throughout the UK, the underlings, the illegals who have been literally shipped here in the knowledge that they'll work for those who funded their trip, would quickly understand that betrayal and independence, has to be and will be punished. It's my understanding that those executing the kidnapping and the killing will be brought in from Albania. They'll be people who will have come in legitimately on a flight, or those from a different part of the UK; even from among those who walked up the beaches of the south coast and who disappeared. Whoever it was, and there would be more than one, they do the job and return either home or into their own world. They are secrets, sleepers who are ready whenever they are called upon."

"Why the foam in the mouth and nose?" Smirthwaite asked. "Never heard of it before in this context."

"Easy, untraceable, effective and cruel."

"Why the change of shoes?" Owen asked. He knew the answer but wanted it explaining to the group. It had taken him some time to comprehend both the cruelty and ingenuity.

"The NCA believes the shoes were a receipt." Cyril pointed to the screen at the far end of the room and then at an officer sitting by the computer to his left. An image of a pair of white training shoes appeared. They were positioned next to a gun, a pile of cash and some bags of cocaine. Inside one of the shoes was a pendant in the shape of what appeared to be two joined guns or a gun filleted, the handles forming two opposing eagle heads reminiscent of the symbol on the Albanian flag. "This is from an Instagram post. The shoes are identical to those taken off Kadare. In fact, close digital forensic analysis says they are the same. The killers deposit those on the body. His shoes are given as a receipt for the money received for doing the job. You can see them here on the second post." He paused as a second image appeared. "This is a later post, a day later, again on the Instagram platform. It proves the job's been carried out. The symbol, the eagle heads, is that of a gang operating within the UK, a gang that is growing quickly. We have confirmed the training shoes in the second photograph were those belonging to Kadare. CCTV from the hotel shows him wearing them the day he went missing and his roommate confirmed the fact."

"It sounds like a bloody game." Smirthwaite did not mince his words.

"Not a game. It's an organised and growing cancer that's already out of control in certain areas. Liverpool is the only major city where Albanian gangs do not flourish. Other gangs have the area as their own territory. The NCA will be leading on this investigation so we move to a support capacity and concentrate on finding Köse and Jones."

There was a pause that brought a degree of discussion but this soon died as the image on screen turned to that of Bernard Jones.

"Our other snared animal is another kettle of fish if you pardon the pun." Cyril turned to April.

April briefed the group on the interview she'd held with Anna Murray.

"It was a random call to the group that instigated the focus of attention on him, a female caller who suggested she'd been abused by him. There was no due diligence done by the group to clarify the information they received, they just instigated the game of snaring the so-called accused, an action they seem to do well. It was the anonymous caller who suggested Jones had been seen with a number of young women and girls at the location too.

You've seen the video taken and sent by ShadowLink and the alleged communication between Jones and what he believed to be an underage girl. You've also seen the photographs he supposedly sent but there's no way as yet they can be corroborated. It's all very insubstantial. It was said that he was somewhat relieved when they told him the interview would not be posted online. I suggest that is not an admission of any form of guilt. Anyone here confronted in such a way would feel the same sense of relief but also a strong fear that they might publish. Whether you're innocent or guilty that would be an extremely and terrifying situation in which to find yourself. Innocent people have committed suicide in similar circumstances. There may well be guilt but who might be the guilty party is still questionable. For the moment we must believe the call was genuine and she is operating a phone selectively. ShadowLink couldn't help there which is no surprise. Jones might also be suffering from guilt but that's an assumption. Your thoughts, please?"

"Someone is making mischief?" Shakti was swift to respond and had chosen her words deliberately.

Cyril turned to April and then to Shakti. "Go on."

"Wife or daughter. Each seems to have an axe to grind."

Stuart Park quickly continued. "They were not alone. Let's not forget Gülen Köse was the last person to be upset by him and the offence was considered sexual abuse although again we found no evidence of this only her word or should I say the word of the owner who found himself without two members of staff. So, if we're talking of mischief ..." He looked at Cyril as he opened a report. Cyril nodded his confirmation for Stuart to continue. "The body parts discovered around town at key locations might fall into that category of being mischievous. We've been talking to experts in the field of sculpture. It was believed from the evidence we had that the head and subsequently the hands were those moulded from Jones himself, maybe even with his consent whether that be currently or in the past we do not know. What we did know was there were the odd traces of a material called alginate which allows moulding to be made from a person but the objects have been viewed by two experts in this field and they both suggest independently they were not. It's believed they were first sculpted in clay and then moulds taken, a traditional process. The end result can then be produced using various materials from plaster or bronze to resin or what we had, PlastSil. We have also been informed that we have what is referred to as a mask rather than a detailed head, making the process a little easier to create.

"The hands, however, were rather more complex and indicate whoever made them had real skill. There are anomalies that were pointed out giving further credence to the manufacturing process. Maybe another bit of mischief, as it can be seen from these expert statements that Jones played no part in the making of these facsimiles. I doubt he even knows they exist. Finally, we can safely assume they were done from personal knowledge of Jones or from good photographs. I'm assured when we find Jones, the mask and hands will not be the correct dimensions."

"Pandora! The word written on the back of the mask," Owen turned to Cyril remembering what he had been told, "was a jar not a box and we have Erasmus to thank for that. What is interesting in light of what's been said is the fact it was a woman, Pandora, who brought evil by releasing what was trapped within." He looked again at Cyril but not for reassurance. His curiosity had been spiked when they had initially discussed the myth and he had done some homework purely out of curiosity. Considering the direction the case was taking, it seemed more relevant than before. "However, she replaced the stopper preventing *hope* from escaping too. The woman who phoned ShadowLink, she also released evil that had haunted her, trapped secrets of her past and to support that she could have been involved in the making and careful placement of the objects? What were they saying to us by placing the mask on a Grecian type jar near the old police station? The hand, were they telling us something about the first forensic lab or the actor who played *The Third Man*, a man who dies but in fact is only missing or are we reading too much into this? And what about the last object found at The Justice Centre. Is that what they are asking for?" He paused allowing his words to sink in. "Or, are we crediting whoever did this with more intelligence than they deserve? Was it Gülen Köse seeking some kind of bizarre retribution? We've heard from her personal tutor and we know she was a skilful sculptor and conveniently she too has buggered off."

"Where's Kerry Jones in all of this? Yes, she's a suspect but we've not discovered her whereabouts even after a thorough search." Cyril's voice did not conceal the degree of frustration he clearly felt. "How can people just disappear? I know it happens, statistically we see that, we've experienced it in the past but it doesn't make it less frustrating. People go and are never seen or heard of again, or maybe we're not doing a good enough job."

"Be careful what you wish for, sir." Shakti raised her

eyebrows and mimed the removal of a cork.

As they left Owen approached Shakti. “Flash’s glass seems half empty today.”

“The contents have bloody evaporated if you ask me! A degree of realism might help him and maybe the rest of us!”

Chapter 15

The vibration of the mobile phone startled Bernard Jones as he sat on the side of the bed, as the last thing he was expecting was a message. The room could not have been described as luxurious but it was practical and the hotel, being part of a chain, offered a degree of comfort and cleanliness. He had booked a stay for three nights under the name of Peters. He had paid in full with cash, explaining that he worked as an expeditor for a civil engineering company and could be called into work at any time, day or night. Sometimes, if there were serious issues he was often required to remain on site for a protracted period of time. He added the words, *for my sins,* which seemed to convince the young woman that the man before her deserved a degree of sympathy. He did not recognise the number and his pulse increased. He answered but said nothing.

"It's me, Kerry. I keep seeing the news. What's happened? Are you alright?"

Bernard did not respond. He held the phone away from his ear.

"Daddy. It's Kerry, Drella. It's me, the girl who beat you at tennis, the girl you ..." She did not finish the sentence. "I thought you'd lost this phone." The voice message on WhatsApp was clear.

He pressed record spoke and released. "I'm fine. Someone said I've been trying to precure girls, I was attacked by one of the groups who threatened to expose me."

"Did you, after all the promises you made to me?"

"No, not this time. I didn't, Kerry. Where've you been? They're looking for you too. That's my fault."

"They'll not find me. I have some help and some financial support. It makes it easier. You can stay with me for a while if it'll help. Where are you?"

***

A call had come into Control during the briefing detailing another possible sighting of Gina May. As with the other caller, Gina May had been seen in the company of a male. Cyril checked the location on Google maps. The couple had been seen the previous evening near the Spa Gardens in Ripon. Running next to the gardens were the extensive grounds belonging to the old Spa Hotel, a building that had stood empty for a considerable time and had been surrounded by plywood hoardings for most of that time. It had been purchased but progress with the renovation had proved slow. Public toilets were situated across the road. Officers had responded and a dog unit was on standby. From all accounts there was no one on site. The likelihood is that the couple would be found inside surrounded by the detritus associated with those living rough. Cyril was assured of his earlier prediction and his mood lifted. The owners had been notified and the security personnel for the building had arrived on site but had been instructed to wait for the police to arrive before searching the interior of the building.

The hoardings were constructed to the edge of Park Street for the length of the building's façade, broken only by the temporary fencing erected across the three entrances to the property. Two police cars had pulled in to the main entrance as an officer walked down the road. A fine drizzle drifted across the street, to investigate Spa Gardens. The area appeared empty but for a woman walking her dog. The other officers waited by the gate. A man, dressed in a fluorescent jacket marked 'Security', appeared from the right of the building as another emerged from the van.

"A colleague is just walking the perimeter of the grounds. We've had kids in before but the CCTV linked to our control room soon stops them in their tracks. The speakers usually scare the shit out of them." He pointed to the cameras positioned on the scaffolding. Cameras seemed to face in all directions and were placed above some horn speakers. "They cover the hoardings and gates. We have others round the back. We rarely get trespassers inside as the lower windows are also boarded up."

The officer in the Spa Gardens made his way to the dividing wall that ran away from the road protected by a row of bushes and trees. He climbed the wall following a semi-beaten track that led to the side of the hotel. Picking his way through the foliage he checked the security of each of the boarded windows. If anyone was going to enter the hotel then this particular area was the most concealed owing to the heavy foliage and the trees, a haven that also offered shelter from the rain. Anyone inside would soon begin to move once they heard his colleagues' voices within the building. He settled down, sheltered further by the eves, and waited.

Another of the officers followed the security guard through the side door. The interior was dark. Most of the original plaster work had been removed bringing an echo and emptiness to the space. Within a minute the temporary stand lights illuminated the room exposing an even bleaker sight to what was once a majestic space. Wires hung from holes within the ceiling giving an even further feeling of desolation.

"Work's stopped for the moment as plans are being finalised. I believe there's been a change of ideas but I'm only security. I've seen plans for the final thing and it'll be bloody brilliant. I know that the initial checks for damp were carried out and treatments completed hence the mess you can see. Upstairs around the roof area has also had remedial work. We get used to it but the end results are always amazing."

They continued the search covering the lower floor rooms deliberately making as much noise as possible. Moving further away from the main area the artificial light soon diminished and both men used torches. It was not long before they heard movement. The officer touched the security man's arm. They stopped, listening to establish the direction of the sounds. The voices, almost whispers, broke the silence. It was difficult orientating the direction of the sound. The officer called the girl's name.

"Gina May?" He waited for a response. There was nothing as the sounds of more frenetic movements were heard. It was clear they were making their move to leave.

The officer positioned by the trees was in the perfect location. Hands emerged around one of the boards securing a small window. It was pushed causing it to fall. A rucksack emerged first, tossed out onto the wet grass followed by the girl. She turned to offer a hand to the lad following. The young man saw the officer first and pulled himself back inside. It was too late for Gina May. The officer had moved quickly and held her by the upper arms. She tried to wriggle but it was only a timid act of defiance. She burst into tears.

"Your parents are worried sick about you, young lady. Do you know that?" His tone left her in no doubt of the severity of her actions. She physically crumbled, only held up by the officer who stumbled slightly as he took her full weight. The scuffle inside told a similar story. There were neither shouts nor sounds of any struggle.

Within five minutes they were seated in the back of separate police cars. The rain had stopped, the sun broke through the clouds as the female officer leaned on the side of one of the vehicles, occasionally looking in at the girl who sobbed and stared across at the boy who continued to look ahead.

"Sad end to Romeo and Juliet. I bet he promised to take her to a posh hotel in Ripon. Wasn't exactly telling lies but … if anything, they look relieved to be where they are. I can think of nothing romantic about dossing in this place overnight no matter what the attraction might be! Maybe I'm just getting too old or becoming cynical about young love!"

The other three officers chuckled as they watched the security detail finish their final checks.

"There's no damage as far as we can see other than compromising the security. Maybe they'll add a camera to the far side of the building."

***

Bernard Jones saw the van pull into the carpark. Kerry had said she would not be present and he was to trust her and the driver called John, just John. He would not be expecting a conversation, he was just doing a job, a favour. Bernard watched as John left the van and lit a cigarette, the sign. He waited a few moments before going across.

"John?" Bernard stood some distance from the van.

John inhaled long and slowly before flicking the remains of the cigarette away and pulling his beanie hat further down his forehead.

"Yep, got it in one. Kerry says you're a shit passenger so you can drive. The gearbox leaves much to be desired but it works. I've got the constitution of an ox so I'll navigate. Driver's seat belt sticks a bit too. You just have to pull it gently." John pushed his glasses up his nose and opened the passenger door. Bernard opened the driver's door and slid in sitting on a piece of flexible pipe.

"Sorry, just throw it into the back. From the vacuum cleaner when I was getting rid of some crap we were carrying earlier."

Jones gently pulled the seat belt, adjusted the mirror and started the van.

***

Cyril read the report and was pleased as well as relieved that his hunch about the girl had been correct. It was a scenario that had been played out from the earliest of times, only these days there was a greater chance the outcome could be more sinister and certainly more tragic. Cyril shook his head as he read that the lad had informed his parents that he was going away walking with a group of mates for four days. He thought of his own parents and the white lies he had fabricated to go to places he should not.

Maxine Geary, the Family Liaison Officer, had escorted the girl home. There would be a fine line to walk for all concerned. There was also assurance needed that Gina May would be safe. It was not unheard of for parents to punish or reject a wayward child.

The photographs and the details for the case were swiftly removed from the whiteboards in the Incident Room. The police website and social media posts would announce that the girl had returned home safely and offer a vote of thanks to the general public for their vigilance and continued support.

"If only every case was as easy as this one," Cyril mumbled as he closed the file. His mind moved on to the thought of the other three missing persons. If he trusted his judgement as he did with the last it should assure him that these people would not be found as easily.

***

The van keys sat where they were left on top of the

polystyrene box. There had been no report of the discovery of the last body part left at the Justice Centre but then that was hardly surprising. Some people in authority would not know or understand the fundamentals of justice if it hit them in the face. Tommy, the cat, purred deeply as a hand ran from his ears and along his back. The satisfying sound seemed to bring with it a calm, a serenity and a change in mood that could only be for the better.

"Everyone should have a Tommy."

The cat's claws extended and sank affectionately into the material and began to pluck the cushion.

"It's not just one trait of yours that I like, Tommy, it's a few. How do I count the ways? I think it's your independence, your selfish unpredictability as well as your ability to charm those around you that I admire equally."

The purring grew louder as if the cat seemed to comprehend fully what had been said.

"Or is it your cruelty when dealing with your chosen prey, be it a bird or a mouse? Or is it the way you torment and taunt the poor creatures, extend their lives just long enough after you've immobilised them before you destroy them without a second thought? But then, Tommy, you kindly deposit them before me, proud and self-congratulatory. Why am I always clearing up somebody else's bloody mess?"

With a degree of tenderness Tommy was lifted from the cushion and placed on the floor. "I need to go to work; a day of anticipation, a day of expectancy and one I have longed for. We have a guest arriving." The cat lolled onto its side, its hind leg extended towards the ceiling as it cleaned the innermost part of its thigh.

The recently acquired old van, the one she always used, was covered with a tarpaulin and positioned in the far corner of the yard close to the small shipping container between the two far buildings. It had been there for two days and she knew that break in use would make starting the engine difficult.

The key turned in the ignition and the motor seemed characteristically more reluctant than usual even though the driver knew it never started on the first attempt.

"Temperamental bitch of a van! I'd swop you for the other if it wasn't nicked and ready." The words were spat with a degree of venom.

The sound of the vehicle entering the yard brought a rush of both nerves and excitement. The room was ready and the kettle was on the stove. "If things go to plan, Tommy, by tomorrow our guest will have been played with and mauled but securely locked in the box. Sadly, he'll be looking a little worse for wear but then we've all been there at some time in our life."

***

Bernard Jones sat on the old mattress, his arms wrapping his legs as he rocked gently. His head still ached and the lump above his right eye seemed swollen. He had just heard what he thought to be a car engine but he could not be sure. The space was silent and dark, a thick blackness seemed to wrap and hold him still, there was no natural light, not even around the door frame. The only illumination would suddenly come from a small and yet powerful LED bulb suspended from the ceiling. That light was intermittent and irregular. There was no switch as far as Jones had been able to see. The light came on at certain times. He had found, after what he considered to be maybe two or three days, neither rhyme nor reason to those times. His concept of day and night had quickly become confused. The light, or the person in charge of it was controlling what circadian rhythm he had and therefore his existence.

He slept for what seemed like moments either sitting or curled in a foetal position. If anything, the artificial day seemed to be extending but even so, it was unnaturally short, as if this new day and night passed too quickly distorting his understanding of his time there. He no longer wore a watch. He neither remembered when that went from his wrist nor when he had arrived in this location. He did, however, remember the group of people who threatened to expose him as a paedophile.

The writing scrawled on the far wall was also real, a wall made of steel and ribbed at regular intervals. The same ribs ran over the ceiling and down the wall he leaned against. When the light allowed, he moved across and touched it, he followed each of the letters with his finger and felt a greater anxiety especially knowing he was in a used shipping container.

PANDORA. The word was written large and seemed to fill the entire centre section of the wall which initially made him think of the containers he had seen displaying *P&O* shipping. For some bizarre reason he tried to visualise the colours of the flag that was set near the script but he failed. The haphazard script was set at an angle and the paint splashed in what appeared to be red; the dribbled runs had travelled to pool on the plywood floor in certain places. The secondary word, *PERVERT* ran vertically from the initial letter until the final letter touched the floor. The sentence, *HOW COULD YOU HARM A CHILD?* ran through the word *pervert* incorporating the latter letter ‘r’. He had read them many times when the light was on and a feeling of fear and revulsion seemed to turn his stomach to a gurgling mulch. His eyes moved to where he knew stood the wooden screen set across a corner, behind which was a camper’s chemical toilet he had used as infrequently as possible. Taped to the screen were some of his own photographs, pictures of him alone and also with Kerry. He had not seen some of them for years. Their presence in this strange space confused and annoyed him. He thought of Kerry, the bedroom, her smile and then that downstairs room, the photographs, the ceramic head and then nothing. He was here.

The most disturbing image was one taken of him with Gülen Köse. It was the largest of the group. He had not been aware it had been taken. Whether that was owing to the angle of the shot or the lack of light when the photograph was taken, he could not determine, but the girl, he knew this girl, she looked frightened and he felt immediate shame.

Without warning the light came on. His eyes stung. Lowering his head, he tried to acclimatise to the lit surroundings as the cat flap in the base of the door opened. A small paper plate appeared holding a sausage roll. There were no words spoken. The flap just closed and the sound of a bolt sliding behind it was all he heard. He had lost count of the number of bits of food he had received in this way, if that is what they could be called. They had been as irregular as the light, the offerings had all been cold and all confectionary, all from a bakery but there had at least been some variety. He knew that within a short time a small bottle of water would also appear.

Counting the paper plates and the bottles that were pushed to the far corner gave no semblance of the time he had been held, if anything they confused his ability to recall anything.

Collecting the plate, he turned to look at the photographs and a question came immediately to mind, it referred to a moment he could never forget.

When was the first time? He tried to recall what she had said in that room when he faced her and asked for forgiveness.

His words were but a whisper but they seemed to echo within the room. "Was she eleven?" Sweat beaded along his forehead even though the room was cool. He wiped them onto the back of his hand. Moving closer to the photographs his finger rested on one taken of Kerry at the tennis club, her face, all smiles as she held the racquet across her chest. He knew the day, he could even tell you the date, he was the proudest man there. Stepping away his breathing changed remembering the self-hatred, the revulsion that hit him when he had shaved the following day and recalled staring at the wet eyes that reflected back, eyes that revealed guilt, disgust and shame. He remembered the promise he had made to himself in full view of the mirror, that it would never happen again, could never happen again; he could not bear to see his child look at him the way she did ... but he did repeat his actions, he could not stop until she said the words he feared to hear.

He threw the plate and contents at the far wall. There was little sound but his action was seen as well as heard and as anticipated, the bottle of water appeared at the bottom of the door.

"If you throw this, Bernard Jones, abuser and user, it will be your last and who knows how long you will be here. We suggest you think before you act. If only you'd done that throughout your adult life ..."

The male voice was unrecognisable. It shook him. Whoever was there watched and heard. The cold reality flushed through him that they controlled him and tears returned as he thought of Kerry.

"Sorry, I am for ... for everything." The words came quickly to his lips but the empathy, the real understanding was clearly lost amongst the sobs.

Chapter 16

Shakti leaned on April's desk. "I visited a college here in Harrogate, I heard of it by pure chance, from my hairdresser. They teach media makeup."

April glanced at her colleague and smiled before looking back at her computer screen.

"That covers the teaching of all aspects of film, television and theatre makeup. Extending that thought, April, it covers horror, hospital and police programmes where you'll see physical injuries that have to look real and very effective under scrutiny." She turned her phone round and showed April some images of the end results of the students' work within the course. "They're so realistic. The zombie was bloody frightening I bet."

"I didn't know this college existed." April flicked the screen looking at each image in turn.

"As I said, I heard about it purely by chance. It doesn't sound like they do any of that stuff from looking at their website as it suggests it's all about health and beauty."

April looked back at the photographs. "To me these seem unhealthy and so bloody ugly!" She laughed. "But clever."

"They have a few linked colleges around the country and the media makeup side is well subscribed. About thirty students within each college study how to make someone look as if they've been hit by a bus. Obviously, with so many new dramas on stream there's a need for creative staff. The latest trend according to a student I spoke to is drag queen makeup!"

April handed the phone back.

"I also spoke with one of the lecturers who was utterly fascinating." Shakti propped her backside on the desk. "In a TV series you can't give the leading detective a black eye and in the next episode have it disappear, no, not at all, the bruising has got to age as in life so the makeup artist has to imitate that change over a realistic time period and it has to look authentic." She paused waiting for a response.

"Fascinating, Shak. And your point is?" A frustration crept into April's voice.

Shakti leaned down and slipped her hand into the bag that rested at her feet and brought out a carrier bag. She tossed it onto the desk deftly avoiding the keypad and mouse. It bounced slightly before landing on April's lap. "You might want to look in there."

April opened the top of the bag and slipped in her hand. "Bloody hell!" She withdrew her hand quickly as she looked at Shakti, her face clearly showing uncertainty and a degree of disgust. "What is it?"

Shakti took the bag and removed the silicone life sized male hand. "Made by the tutor as a film prop. Reminds me of the objects found at three of our locations. I've borrowed it. This is even more life-like as it's coloured to give a more realistic appearance of a severed hand. However, there's an important question we need to consider. Ask me how much it would cost to make." She offered it back to April who reluctantly took it whilst at the same time pulling a face. "Go on. Ask!"

"How much to make it?" Her voice was flat offering little enthusiasm for the conversation.

"£300 plus."

April's face demonstrated incredulity. "What! For this?"

Shakti nodded. "Those three items we found will have an approximate cost to the maker of over a grand, a thousand pounds, April. Who has that sort of money to make them and then leave them around the place where they could just be taken and if they can afford to do it, why? Why not just leave photographs, why specific false body parts we believe to be modelled from Bernard Jones that cost a fortune?"

"Could his daughter, Kerry, have been involved in the college course or could she know someone who was?" April turned the prosthesis in her hands but this time she looked at it with greater interest. "If the material came through illicit college stock or a legitimate project then that would clearly reduce the cost to the person leaving it to be negligible."

"I spoke with the lecturer and they take full and part time students but for the making of prosthetics such as those they would have to be at Level Four standard. They've put time in and passed exams. What's important is the skills and with skills comes either jobs on the side or sharing of those skills for something in return." Shakti edged further onto the desk. "A foreigner in trade's speak."

"Let's look at this new information in the light of what we already have." April crossed the room and dragged a flip chart back. She picked up a pen and began writing as she spoke. "Gülen Köse, is a skilled sculptor, we know from images of her work and her personal tutor's comments, we also know she was working in Harrogate illegally and made protestations about Bernard Jones that were of a sexual nature. Kerry Jones, is missing but from what we know from her mother she is not Bernard Jones's daughter. We need to ask ourselves a key question, Shak. Why did she leave home after her mother left? What went on? In the light of Jones being snared by ShadowLink we can make an uncomfortable assumption that maybe she was abused in some way by him. We know that she's manipulative after she discovered her mother having sex. What else did she witness and whom else did she try to blackmail?"

"Two women both linked to Jones, both missing, both may have been sexually harassed. Neither woman we can predict is flush with cash and therefore this information opens and yet swiftly closes certain avenues." Shakti picked up a marker pen before adding a large question mark to the chart.

"Did you receive a list of the students who studied this specific course? Most are likely to live locally if there are colleges dotted around the country, students as you say who have achieved the necessary skill set or are close to achieving it?" April paused as the thoughts surfaced quickly. "We can assume there might have been a name change as we're thinking of Kerry, Köse wouldn't be part time at any college now not having a visa. The college will probably keep photo ID, I feel sure, as they will all wear ID lanyards."

"Our facial recognition software should sort that

relatively quickly." Shakti lifted her police lanyard. "It seems compulsory in most higher education establishments that students have these."

"GDPR will help make the task that bit more difficult but the official request has been submitted," April announced, a degree of frustration clearly visible.

***

Jones sat once again in the dark. The light seemed to be on for less than an hour at a time and as soon as it was extinguished the voice spoke as he stumbled his way to the sanctuary which was the only furnishing, the single mattress positioned on a plastic sheet and then a large wooden pallet.

"What's the worst thing for you at the moment, Bernard?" The following pause seemed as black and sticky as his surroundings.

His breathing seemed inordinately loud and he tried to control it and bring his anxiety under control.

"It's the not knowing, isn't it? The not knowing when it will come on again, if it will stay on but then, even worse, I feel sure, is the question you face, when will it go off, go off and leave you completely in the dark? In the dark physically and metaphorically. Is that correct, Bernard?" The silence came again. Bernard felt his head nodding the answer, no words seemed to come. "The girls felt just that. When will it happen again, when will he come, when will the hurt enter my room, spoil my life? It's the not knowing, the not being in control, the impotence that hangs in their heads like the deepest darkness. I control the light and the dark of your now small world, the uncertainty and anxiety, you unknowingly controlled theirs. Just the two, or we hope and believe there were only two but who knows? The others might be hidden in the dark, afraid to speak out, afraid to tell the truth. That's what happens, you see, Bernard. They tell me that you slowly but surely suffocate them with an insidious fear and it takes a brave young woman to break away or stand in the way of such abuse. They have, Bernard, they did and you then had to look elsewhere."

Bernard Jones had cupped his hands over his ears in an act of denial.

"Kerry was here, I saw her, she asked me to come. She held the racquet. She was dressed in white. She called me, said she would help. I came. I saw her."

"You saw her, Bernard?"

"I fucking saw her!" He screamed back his voice quivering and breaking midway into a high pitch squeal. "And she did this!" He pointed to his head.

"Are you sure? Or was it someone who looked like her? The mind can play such dreadful tricks when it's confused. Were you confused, Bernard? Remember, you saw John too. Did you recognise John?"

There was silence.

"How old is the girl you believed to be your daughter? Remember, she's no longer a girl, is she, Bernard? She's a young woman, a scarred young woman, angry at what you did, what her mother did. She no longer wears the white tennis skirt you so much liked, she's older, she's no longer like the photograph you stare at constantly." The light came on. "Take a look, go on. It always turned you on that sight. It has the same power as I to turn off this light. Do you remember the prom dress, her hair and makeup? Do you remember what you wanted and you were denied?"

"Shut up! I was sorry, she knew I was sorry. I've said that over and over again. She promised to help. My daughter, my Cinderella said she could ..."

Immediately the darkness returned.

"I saw her, she wanted my help. She said so. Please, give me some light!"

Chapter 17

Cyril held the prosthetic hand. He had checked the cost of materials in retrospect. Nobody, including himself, had considered the cost of producing such an item. He held it next to a photograph of the last body part found. The scale ruler positioned alongside gave him an approximate measure of the object.

"I spoke with the tutor responsible for teaching this stuff again today. She herself has worked on many television dramas where these and other prosthetic effects are commonly used. There are various qualities of the silicone they use too. She tells me that the high-grade silicone you'll find in cooking utensils, bun cases and the like. She confirmed the specialist products are going to be expensive." Shakti took the hand. "I have to return it today as she's doing a presentation tomorrow and this is one of her props."

Cyril raised his eyebrows. "We have a chemical analysis of the material and we'll try to track company sales but that's a long shot at present."

"We checked the ages of the students studying media makeup and then ran their photographs. We only had one possible match for Kerry Jones but further investigation suggests it's not her. This girl still lives at home here in Harrogate with her parents. Still nothing from the public after running Kerry's photograph across all the channels. We've not been able to get full parental co-operation with the pleas for help, her mother still wants nothing to do with it but we persevere." Shakti leaned back in her chair. "She's just one of many young people who've gone missing that are never seen again."

"It's not surprising," April responded. "We get so few responses apart from those who enjoy wasting police time. If you think of the number of people you walk past every day and never give them a second glance it's understandable. Then, Shak, if the missing person is out of context or has changed their appearance by any means … we're just so lucky we found the other girl. Did you see the CCTV from The Justice Centre?"

Shakti nodded.

"It captured the person leaving the hand but from the way they positioned their face they knew the camera was there. We have an approximate height and some details of clothing but they'll be in a charity bag by now. There's more, from gait analysis the person is said to be female, about five feet five in height and of medium build."

Shakti frowned. "That's close enough for Kerry Jones but also probably for forty-five percent of the female population in this town."

Grimshaw moved through the office and called April's name before handing an A4 sheet of paper to each officer. On it he had written three headings:

Old Police Station
Old Forensic Lab
Justice Centre

"I was sitting with a pint last night and I couldn't get these locations out of my mind. So much so, I walked to each one before returning for another drink. The first thing that struck me was the proximity of each location. Ironically, Robert Street is central within the triangle the route makes." He suggested they look at the street map on one of the walls before tracing the route he had walked with his finger. "There's Cyril's place, that fact is really quite irrelevant but it did amuse me. However, there was a serious side to this and the location proximity might be relevant. Imagine you're a young woman who's faced some kind of abuse in her early life. What's the first action you'd take?"

April frowned before looking at Shakti. "Are you serious, Dan?"

Grimshaw nodded. "Even more so now, stick with me but be honest and serious. This isn't a joke."

"If it's serious abuse and not child petulance then the young person should seek help from their parents."

"Right! But if it's the parents or parent who's committed the abuse. What then?"

"The police?" Shakti snapped back. "It might also be picked up at school or maybe someone they can trust, someone responsible."

Grimshaw nodded, turned the sheet he was holding to face the women and pointed to the first heading. "Indeed. Now, if the police became involved and sexual impropriety was suspected. What then?"

"Forensic tests."

"Correct."

He pointed to the second heading. "And the last heading?"

Shakti leaned forward. "It goes to court or justice is sought and hopefully received which should end the abuse and the perpetrator receives punishment?"

"I came to those same conclusions. I thought of Kerry Jones but I checked and there's no record on file of any recorded abuse with us or any case linked with Child Protection Services. I had a word with one of the Safeguarding Team and it was quite an eye opener. Most child sexual abuse isn't reported, detected or prosecuted at the time and those three words fit perfectly into my headings. The information stopped me in my tracks. The kids don't go to the police therefore no investigation forensically or otherwise takes place and no prosecution can occur, in other words, justice cannot be served. Also, a child does not know that the behaviour of an adult they trust, in many cases the parent, is abuse and they say nothing or they may be too afraid to say anything."

"You're suggesting it's a delayed cry for help, Dan?"

"That's always a possibility but no, on the contrary. I think it's a cry and I believe it to be a scream of anger. To me, it's revenge and quite possibly catharsis. It's about highlighting and then closing down the past. The locations are all from the town's past. The station, the Otley Road building and yet the Justice building is relatively new. Is justice going to be delivered and if so, how? We've seen the video from the hunter group. They've told us of a report. I'm truly concerned for the wellbeing of Bernard Jones."

"Why not leave the objects at this station?"

"We bristle with CCTV. The past is the past apart from the last location. They knew the risks of placing the hand at the justice centre. However, it was a risk worth taking to meet their agenda."

Nothing was said as this information was digested.

***

The noise of the diesel engine starting up seemed to send a vibration through the metal walls of the room. Jones felt it, the surface he was leaning against shook briefly and then settled to what seemed like a permanent shiver. The sudden change from the general silence and dark calm to the constant deep thrum brought an initial curiosity but then this was quickly replaced by uncertainty and fear. Bernard Jones moved away from the wall and lay on the mattress, his legs tucked tightly to his chest. He said nothing, he had tried shouting but he had never received a response.

Had the light been on he may have noticed the vent positioned near to the floor behind the screen and the chemical toilet. It was painted the same colour as the metal walls and blended perfectly, a vent that allowed air to flow into the container. Its role had now been changed. Taped to the back of the container vent was a flexible pipe, a combination of three old vacuum cleaner hoses. They ran away and connected to an adapted exhaust of the single cylinder diesel generator. The length allowed significant cooling of the gases before entering the vent. The generator was old and importantly contained no catalytic convertor. That fact significantly increased the toxicity of the exhaust fumes. The battered generator sat on a plastic-covered wooden pallet some distance from the container. With the fuel capacity at its maximum, it could run for up to twelve hours. That timespan would not be needed.

Jones was wrapped in his own mental struggle, a cocktail of guilt and anxiety and this mental fight distracted him from the changes that were occurring, the darkness concealed any visible trace of the fumes leaching into his space, the silent killer that would soon bring him to his senses before quickly removing them. The LED light would not come on again and he would hear nothing more from the male voice.

The stench, the choking, the treacly fumes hung around the floor, the silent tsunami began creeping into each corner and flowed effortlessly over every obstacle. Jones felt it first in his throat and he began to cough. He tucked himself more tightly into a ball unaware of the cause. Within minutes his cough grew worse and his head began to throb. He sat up, immediately feeling some relief. He breathed more deeply as if to expunge whatever was causing the sudden coughing spasm. It was then the nausea came, light at first and not too dissimilar to motion sickness which he had often experienced. The more deeply he inhaled the greater the nausea. His breathing grew shallow and he began to sweat, the same sweat he had experienced from his feelings of guilt.

Leaning a hand on the metal wall he stood. The faint vibration was still present but now he thought nothing of it. His main concern was breathing. He vomited once and then quickly a second time covering most of the mattress. His head pounded as his breathing grew more eager and shallow. If only he could see, if only he could think more clearly. A fear stabbed at his heaving stomach.

"Help! Somebody," his voice sounded feeble and pathetic.

The generator continued to beat out a constant rhythm whilst pumping more exhaust into the metal cage. It was quickly poisoning Bernard Jones. Now on his knees he vomited one more time, the acidic taste filling his throat, mouth and nostrils. The pounding in his head grew more severe and he lay down on the mattress and curled into the foetal shape yet again. His attempts to draw in clean air began to slow and a calm, a peace seemed to flush through his body. It suddenly seemed alright to relax, to close his eyes, to rest. The nausea had passed, the throbbing in his head diminished. He was going to be fine. The blackness of his surroundings crept into his thoughts. He could not feel any part of his body, each limb failed to respond when he tried. That was fine. He seemed to be so light as if floating, suspended and above the room. Even with his eyes closed he looked at the shape curled on the mattress below, a shape that looked familiar but a body that looked at peace.

***

The generator motor had ticked for some time whilst cooling as the doors to the container were opened. Fresh air flushed the interior ridding it of the fumes. Natural light flooded the space. Bernard Jones's body lay semi-curled as if he were sleeping, still positioned on the mattress. The Fiat van he had driven to get there was parked close by, the rear doors opened exposing the empty interior.

The yard was quiet and private as the forklift manoeuvred along the two gradient ramps linking the yard to the container's internal wooden floor, enabling the truck to enter the stepped doorway. The driver lowered the twin forks and moved forward slipping them beneath the mattress and into the opening of the wooden pallet. With one movement of the lever, the body, mattress and pallet rose about a metre before the forklift backed down the ramp, turned and moved towards the rear of the van. As it braked, Jones's limp arm flopped from the side of the mattress. Within seconds a gloved hand had repositioned it.

The pallet entered the van slowly until it reached the slatted metal screen behind the driver's seat separating the rear from the cab. There was minimal clearance between the protruding internal wheel arches but by tipping the forks, the plastic and mattress holding the body slid onto the van's deck as the pallet was carefully extracted.

Looking in, Jones appeared as though he were still sleeping. A pool of fluid from the vomit that covered some of his clothing, the sleeve, hand and most of the mattress brought with it a nauseating stench. Soon it would be confined within the van. It would grow even stronger once the doors were closed.

The van, stolen some weeks before, had sat beneath a tarpaulin in the corner of the yard. A solar battery trickle charger had been connected as additional security. It would start when needed.

***

A large floodlight positioned on one of the walls illuminated the yard giving the surroundings a jaundiced appearance. The van containing the body remained where it had been loaded. It still had a sheen from the water used to wash the paintwork. The driver crossed the yard, wiped his feet on an old piece of carpet positioned near the driver's door before entering. The only person to drive since Jones was always dressed from head to foot in protective clothing. Jones had been guided to park it close to the container. He'd been confused until he looked across the yard at someone waving.

The driver's seat had not been cleaned. The fact that Bernard Jones had last driven the van last was key; his fingerprints and DNA were now present throughout the cab.

Once the driver was in, shoe protectors were slipped on. The steering wheel was covered in a protective sleeve, normally used in garages as a precaution when mechanics are dealing with customer's cars. The gear shift was also protected. Any ancillary switches would not be used for this run other than the lights, they would be left on along with the engine when the vehicle was finally parked.

The van started on the first turn of the key emitting a cloud of black and then grey smoke along with the initial engine rattle. Within two minutes another van pulled out behind. It was hoped that with driving on country roads, the darkness and careful driving, the stolen vehicle would not be spotted now the original number plates had been uncovered.

***

Dr Callum Shaw pulled over to the side of the road and

parked. He was early. The morning was warm but the dawn's layer of light grey clouds concealed the sun. The lack of sunshine had not prevented him from buying an ice cream from the Ripley ice cream parlour next to the store even though he had not yet eaten breakfast, after all he was on holiday. Although he had worked only an hour's drive away when in Leeds he had never been to the village before but what he saw he admired. There was an old-world charm making him believe he had walked onto a film set. The pub seemed to dominate the centre of the village. It was masked by a creeper that clung to The Boar's Head pub façade but the plant was tamed with skill, ensuring the foliage followed the windows and the pub sign with precision. The cobbled area to the front of the building enhanced its authenticity and beauty.

A stone sculpture of a resting wild boar had drawn his attention and he crossed the road to inspect the finer details. It was partially encased in wrought iron railings and at each front corner were stone bowls set below brass taps. He assumed they were positioned to offer water to horses or dogs. With an artist's eye he studied the intricate, carved detail.

"Couldn't sleep like me, I take it." The voice from behind startled him. An elderly gent wearing tweeds and a flat cap moved to stand next to him before pointing a walking stick at the boar. "From the king that is. Not that statue, that came here as a gift to this village in 1907 if my memory serves me well. No, I'm talking way back in time, Thomas Ingleby, who lived in the castle down yonder," the stick waved again below his nose and Shaw obediently followed the direction indicated. "He was hunting with King Edward the Third in Knaresborough Forest and the king fell off his horse, the clumsy sod. Anyroad, an injured boar was about to gore him as he lay on the ground but it was killed by Thomas Ingleby, yon mon who lived in the castle yonder." He pointed the stick again. "You can imagine the King was grateful and he knighted Thomas and allowed him to use the boar's head on his crest. That's why you'll see the critters everywhere in the village, hence the pub name too. We also have wonderful ice-cream but I can see you've discovered that," he looked at the cone. "Just thought you'd like to know a bit of the history." He lifted his cap and headed towards the church. The sound of an aircraft, faint but near caused him to search the sky but to no avail.

Patting the stone boar on the head he spoke out loud. "If you'd have had your way that day, piggy, I wonder who'd be on the English throne now?" Shaw lifted the remaining cone to his lips as another hand touched his shoulder. He recognised the perfume and remained looking at the statue.

"You're early."

Turning, he looked at the woman before him. "Eager, not early. There's a subtle difference." He glanced at his car and noticed a van had parked behind.

"How did you get here?"

"I have a friend to thank for that."

If Callum Shaw had seen the casual observer sitting on a bench outside The Boar's Head, he showed little interest. Why should he, this was his first visit. Had he done so he would have recognised the person. His mind was racing with a degree of excitement for what the rest of the day had to offer.

"What have you planned?" The excitement in his voice

was clear. "I was so thrilled you called me."

"A walk down to the lake as the weather's fine, the castle had been my choice had it been raining and then possibly lunch if you're feeling generous and then there's the gallery over there, I thought you'd like that." Her smile was as he remembered. He could never quite discern its sincerity unless she broke into a laugh. It was tight and a little too swift to disappear.

"Which way?" Callum tossed what was left of the ice-cream into a bin.

She slid her arm in his and they headed down Holybank Lane, past the church and the castle and onto the footpath. There were a number of walkers who greeted them with smiles and passed the occasional time of day.

"I never thought I'd see you again after the last time." He paused but did not turn to look at her. "I was sorry about that. I thought …" He stopped himself from continuing as he felt he was digging himself into a deeper hole that could only end one way, resulting in a few minutes of uncomfortable silence.

"I trusted you and you let me down. I received your messages, all of your messages and the photographs." A broader smile came to her face and she raised a hand. "Some were, shall we say ..." Her facial expression changed as she removed her arm from his and deliberately put some space between them. The significance of this deliberate withdrawal did not go unnoticed by the person walking some distance behind. It was as if it were a pre-arranged signal. The figure stopped, watching briefly for the next sign. It came as she moved back and linked Callum Shaw's arm again. There was no reason to observe any more just a desire to get back and wait.

Chapter 18

"We're needed. We have a potential suicide. Bernard Jones."

"Are we certain it's Jones? Suicide, are you sure, Owen?" Cyril immediately thought of the silicone face purporting to be Jones and alarm bells began to ring in his head.

"Seems so. It's the common one, pipe up the old exhaust and into the car. All over red rover! If it's true what the group insinuated, it's a coward's way out if you ask me. It seems to have been effective." Owen moved away from the architrave releasing more light into the room.

Cyril dropped his glasses onto his desk. "Where?"

"West Gate carpark near the entrance to Fountains Abbey, in a stolen vehicle taken from Chapel Allerton, that's north Leeds." He looked up and saw the frown on Cyril's face that told him he was telling him something he already knew.

"I know it's in bloody Leeds, Owen. Go on."

"According to witnesses, and the person who reported the discovery, the van was parked there very early in the morning or at some time during the night. It's positioned at the far end and furthest from the road, an area that can't be seen from the road. The engine wasn't running when discovered but the officers who were first on the scene were confident it had run until the fuel had run out. The bonnet was still warm and it was hot inside. None of the doors was locked. The key was still in the ignition. There was a pipe running from the exhaust through to the passenger window that was wound up trapping a quantity of the pipe inside the van. All of this should have been easily seen but the van was backed up to foliage and the passenger side was tight to the border hedging. Ambulance called and risk assessments, I've been informed, have been carried out. Considering the Overstone Criteria and the info we hold on Jones I've asked for a cordon, CSI and crime scene log starting."

"Good man. It sounds just too perfect, Owen, it has all the makings of a suicide, wife left him for another bloke, daughter left under strange circumstances and it wasn't reported at the time, discovered daughter was not his and then he was confronted by the paedophile hunter group. Someone would just want us to encourage the coroner to close it down but, my dear friend, something just doesn't feel right and we haven't even visited the scene yet." Cyril wanted to use the term *crime scene* but thought better of it. "I want someone handling the press. You know how they can blow these things out of all proportion. Low key, Owen, low key until we know what we're looking at."

***

As Cyril's car approached the scene down Fountains Abbey

Lane an officer was waiting in the road. Owen briefly flicked on the blue lights concealed within the grille and the windscreen and was directed into the carpark entrance. The police tape was in place a short distance from the road. In front of that a police car was parked across the carpark, its door open. An officer climbed out and approached Cyril passing the fast response paramedic's vehicle that was parked to the left.

"Confirmed dead, sir." He turned to look at the paramedic. All the signs of suic …"

Cyril held up his finger stopping the officer in midflow.

"Remember your A, B and C in cases such as these. Assume nothing, believe nobody, and challenge everything."

The officer pulled a face and looked at the paramedic.

"You can believe him if he's told you he's dead but at this stage that's all. Is there a note or letter in the vehicle?"

"We looked but unless it's under the mattress we couldn't find one. He seems to have vomited a lot. I think they do in these circumstances. There's a small photograph in one corner of the van. It was face down. Looks like a girl in tennis gear but it's heavily soiled. How a victim can stay enclosed when they're going through that is a mystery to me. They choke to death when all they need to do is open the bloody door."

"Most people would be mystified, too. Desperation is a dreadful thing." Cyril wanted to add the word *guilt* but thought better of it. Looking at the officer's age he assumed it was the first time he had witnessed a sudden and unexplained death.

"Are you sure about the photograph?"

"Would you care to look, sir? It's a bit messy."

The thought of body fluids spread liberally within a contained space held no fascination for Cyril, they had always repulsed him even as a small child. Body fluids were his bête noire, particularly his own. He shook his head.

"Minimum footfall in the area. Let's wait for the CSI to do their thing. Any cameras?"

The officer pointed to the sign at the entry to the carpark. It's the carpark prioritising the disabled and it says that CCTV is in operation. I've looked. I thought that was one but it's a floodlight, I can't see any cameras."

Cyril was aware that it would be easy to jump to the conclusion of suicide and considered the appropriate response in the circumstances. Everything pointed in a certain direction but he was aware murder could be easily camouflaged. His actions, at this stage, should be unbiased and non-judgemental. The evidence that would be found should point him to a verdict. Right at this moment it was suspicious and he wanted to file that with the coroner once he was fully aware of the facts from Forensics.

Within minutes the CSI van arrived alongside another police vehicle. The CSI came over to the cordon and looked across at the van as if mentally calculating what was needed. She then approached Cyril.

"You seem to get the good jobs, Detective Chief Inspector. I saw Owen when we were turning in and expected you to be nearby." She glanced over to the van. "Has there been much foot traffic do you know?"

"Person who discovered it very early on and then the paramedic there and the two officers. They know the rules. They threw a cordon across immediately as this place can get busy. I believe traffic is being stopped on Abbey Road and anything from here directed that way until this is cleared."

"I'm CSM and we'll get started if your lads can keep the prying eyes of Joe Public and if possible, the press at bay. I'll keep you posted." She smiled and walked back to her van, chatted briefly with her colleague before applying PPE.

***

Cyril sat in the car and watched as the CSI moved around the vehicle using step plates. The rear doors had been checked. The van would be going for full forensic investigation depending on the initial findings. Owen opened the driver's door.

"One of the lads has brought some coffee from the café up the road way, part of the Abbey." He handed Cyril a polystyrene cup wrapped in a corrugated sleeve. "It says the contents are hot so be careful. We live in a bloody nanny state." He shook his head. Owen took a careful sip. "That's wrong as it's bloody lukewarm. However, it's wet."

Cyril looked at it, also took a sip and handed it straight back. "I'll pass. I could offer a better description but it would be wasted on you, Owen, but thank you."

Cyril climbed from the car as he saw the CSM approach. She pulled down her hood and dropped her mask.

"Is it straightforward enough for us all to go home?" He kept a straight face.

"Strange one, if I'm honest. The space within the van is limited. A man could not stand or even kneel without hitting the roof and yet ..."

Cyril moved closer. "And yet?"

"His vomit has travelled further than I'd expect from a person in a recumbent position. It's all over the mattress but more importantly it's also between him and the mattress. I'd expect some ingress if he rolled in his final death throes but we're talking, how shall I put this delicately, the more solid residue is clearly still there."

It was important for him to hear this initial evidence but he did not appreciate the fine detail.

"Why have a mattress in the back of a van that I believe is stolen, unless it was there when it was taken, or it's been planned to suggest suicide? But then why have the mattress on plastic sheeting?"

Cyril looked straight at her. He did not want to sway her decision either way. She was the expert and these initial impressions would be the key to what happened next.

"There looks to be wood splinter residue on the underside of the plastic sheet. We can only see around the edges as yet but it's there. We'll know more when the van is back at the lab where it can be scrutinised. One other thing, the photograph that was in there does not appear to have been held after he vomited."

Cyril was mystified by her eye for detail and it was clearly reflected in his expression.

"How do I know? I hear you thinking," she laughed. "We have ways! I know the officer picked it up but in my opinion the chap in the van didn't. As I said, we'll also know more when it's back with us. One other thing. I've checked and photographed the soles of his shoes. Just look at yours now."

Cyril tipped his shoe. It was covered with a layer of soil from the carpark.

“His shoes are not soil free but they don’t contain this soil and I know he doesn’t hover.”

“Can you say it’s suicide?” Cyril had really heard enough.

“Situations like this are difficult as there were no witnesses. The person jumping from a bridge or the one stepping deliberately in front of a train, that’s fairly straightforward. Circumstances such as these are not and we should not judge them too quickly. There are three things that make the alarm bells ring. Why leave a perfectly good driver’s seat and curl up in the back? Why try to conceal the pipe against hedges? If he drove here in the dark, who’s going to see him sitting behind the wheel? Within thirty minutes he’s going to be unconscious and more than likely dead. The shoes really crown it for me at the moment. There’s enough from what I see to believe that it’s not clear cut, there’s a degree of suspicion to say it wasn’t suicide. Further investigation might prove that theory to be wrong, we’ve been wrong in the past, but at this moment from what I’ve seen …” she rocked her hand to demonstrate a degree of deliberation was still needed. “That’s my professional judgement at this stage, sorry if that doesn’t help.”

“Thanks. My gut had a similar feeling.”

“Are you sure it wasn’t all that talk of vomit.” She smiled and cocked her head to one side.

“Maybe. My reputation goes before me I see.” Cyril needed to treat this as a possible murder enquiry. The coroner would be notified.

"I've left instructions for the van to be collected once we've done what we can and he's removed."

"Any sign of a mobile phone?"

"His jacket was stuffed in the passenger window but the pockets were empty. Trouser pockets are clear too. There's nothing. No money, cards, wallet. No watch either. Some suicides do that, they throw away the life that has brought them to this point."

"We've not been able to find his phone and there's been no calls made or received since the day he was stopped by the paedophile group but I'm aware with today's technology there are other ways of hidden communication. There's also been no card transactions, no digital trail."

"If this was planned, as I said, those who dilly-dally on the edge of criminality prepare, store cash, make provision by having an escape route. Squirrels, Cyril or maybe even boy scouts. Be prepared. Dib, dib, dib."

"Dilly-dally. Right, thanks. I'll await your findings." He brought his hand to the side of his head holding two fingers straight in a scout's salute.

***

Dr Callum Shaw brought out the two drinks from the side door of The Boar's Head followed by one of the staff who carried two plates of sandwiches. They'd chosen a bench facing what appeared to be a pillar surmounted by a stone block, the village stocks were to the other side.

"One cheese and one ham." He squeezed onto the bench that was attached to the table. "There are rumours of some police incident near Fountains this morning."

"Really? I'm starving." She picked up the sandwich and started to eat. "Do you really want to visit the gallery after this or do you want to see where I'm now living?" She turned to Shaw and raised an eyebrow. The sound of sirens travelling along the bypass made them both turn in the direction. The wail convinced her she needed to move and move quickly.

The suggestion brought a flutter to his stomach. "It seems so long since … I don't need to look at paintings, I'm surrounded by them every day. May I take your photograph? It's such a beautiful spot."

The shake of the head in combination with the frown told him everything he wanted to know.

The van that was parked behind Shaw's car had gone. As he pulled out onto the Ripley bypass he followed the verbal instruction he was given.

"It's not far. You'll love it, bit untidy mind. It's on a farm. It's quite remote and sometimes smells a bit but I love it. The building was obsolete and neglected when it and the surrounding farm land were taken over by a large farming conglomerate. They rented out the farm house. A few of us got together to do it up with what we could afford so don't think it's like something from those posh house mags, it's not but it's home and a part of it is mine." She turned to look at him. "A bedroom and bathroom!" She glanced sideways, smiled before wrapping her arms around herself.

"Home is where the heart is. I've always believed that." He paused thinking about what she had said. "Is the rest deserted?"

"Some of the larger buildings, like the barns are used. They store machinery for long periods, the harvester and other bits and bobs but I don't know what they do. We hardly see anyone other than when they collect or return them, usually at unearthly hours. For me it's a place where I can hide away from the world when I want to and all the shit that goes with it and I've known shit."

Shaw turned and looked at his passenger. She had not really changed, if anything she was a lot less bolshy and a little more mature but there was still the same vulnerability and that warmed him. His mind went back to the first time he had met her. He tried to think of the year. He had liked her then; he admired her spirit and her no nonsense love of life. He remembered the darkness too, the depressive moods that seemed to come for no apparent reason and the accompanying anger.

"Next left and then right after about half a mile. Do you always drive like a geriatric?"

"Safely you mean?"

"You buy a flash car ... what is it a Jag?"

"A Lexus and it's not flash, it's practical."

"You buy a not so flash, practical car and drive it as if you're ninety."

She added a childlike voice and it brought another flutter to his stomach. He laughed. "Do you want to drive?"

"Nope. I want to sit here and count every fucking blade of grass, which I can do at this speed." She glanced at her watch.

"Here. Turn here."

The lane was narrow and rutted where heavy farm vehicles had corrugated the track into two parallel lines leaving a mound of grass centrally.

"We turn off into the yard very soon. It's on your left

after that tree."

The Lexus slowed to almost a stop. The turn was tighter than he had expected and the car ran close to a derelict drystone wall and a gate post that leaned away from the track.

"They don't get a combine down here surely?" Shaw breathed as he continued to negotiate the narrow lane.

"Nope, they go further and turn in to the yard at the top. This is for those who can drive." She pulled a face but did not look at him.

Within a minute the buildings came into view.

"There's a blue shipping container in the yard. You can park near there, just don't block the doors. They should be open."

The yard was quiet and Shaw pulled up away from the container. The Dutch barn to his right was filled with large round straw bales wrapped in black plastic. Wooden pallets were stacked to one side. He climbed out. A rural aroma greeted him. It was not unpleasant. A van was parked within the second barn next to a yellow combine and an old forklift truck. He looked twice at the van. He was sure he had seen it somewhere before.

"Like it?" Her words interrupted his musings and she moved over and slid her arm into his. "I told you it was a bit run down but it's a world away. If I could only have enjoyed a place like this when I was a kid. Come on, I need a coffee and you need to meet Tommy."

Callum Shaw turned immediately. "Tommy?"

"You'll see. He's a bit like you. Knows what he wants and usually gets it."

Chapter 19

Who would do it and why? I see the motive to end his life and I understand what might have been the tipping point. Cyril tapped his pen against his teeth as if to aid his thought processes as he stared at the details on the Incident Room wall. The latest news had increased the activity of those colleagues present and the hum of conversation could be heard but not enough to distract his pondering. What did, however, was the welcome rattle of the cup in the saucer as Owen approached. Cyril half expected an announcement that *two soups* were to be served. He could imagine Julie Walters' shaky delivery of the two words. April had found the sketch for him to watch on his computer after he had mentioned the problem he always faced with Owen's disastrous delivery of a cup of tea.

"Resisted filling it too full as it floods the saucer, sir. A tip from April. Thing is though, you only get a gob full. But china it must be." He stuffed his hand in his pocket and brought out a chocolate digestive, inspected it and handed it to Cyril before retrieving his own.

Cyril held it at arm's length between his finger and thumb and rotated it slowly. "Could you eat two, Owen?"

Owen had popped the whole biscuit into his mouth. "Are you sure?"

The words came along accompanied by a fusillade of minute, partially masticated biscuit that thankfully landed just short of Cyril's cup. Owen's hand swiftly reached to take the offered confectionery.

Cyril thought it wise to wait until the second digestive had been well washed down with tea before asking his question.

"You saw the scene, Owen, and you've seen enough suicides and murders to make an informed judgement. What's your opinion?"

Cyril pointed to a flow chart he had attached to the whiteboard entitled, *Dealing with sudden unexpected death.* It showed the process for potential suicide investigations. He had positioned it next to the photographs of the silicone body parts found at the three locations.

"It's good to refresh our thoughts on this advice. What my gut says is irrelevant if we don't have the evidence to back it up. What we do have, however, is experience and a vast amount of information from which we can make the judgement as quickly as possible and that counts for a lot in these circumstances."

"It's either murder or aided suicide. Maybe whoever did this gave him little choice. A threat of exposure or …" Owen spoke with conviction.

"Why would they leave these?" Cyril tapped the photographs. "They're clearly of Jones."

"I go along with Dan Grimshaw's theory. It's a belated form of retribution. If the person were a child when he did what he did, then to wait until you've the means and maturity, would be understandable."

"Kerry Jones? Is that who you think?"

"Yes, but not on her own. She'd never stand a chance but with some of those people from within a hunter group like ShadowLink, then anything's possible. They can be intelligent, determined and ruthless. We've seen that in the past. Vigilante justice has always gone on and always will. Sometimes we've seen them persecute and kill the wrong person. Then there's Gülen Köse, she was skilled enough to have created the silicone bits, allegedly she was also abused by Jones. What else did he have on her? Did he know she didn't have a visa? Did he in fact get her the job? What was their relationship before she worked there? He worked in Leeds at some stage so did their paths cross then? There's one thing, the Turks have family all over the place and I imagine she has relatives, cousins and the like living here. They would see wrongs righted. We've seen it before. She'd not need to rely on ShadowLink."

"You should eat more digestive biscuits, Owen." Cyril finished his tea. "I have a huge nag about one thing over all else. How did the person, who ever it might be, know about the location of the first forensic lab? I bet ninety-eight percent of those living in Harrogate have no idea that the first forensic lab in the north east was in that house on Otley Road. There's no plaque like on many other buildings of significance. It's like the Brunswick Tunnel or The Harrogate Club, they're there but not many know it. If it were Kerry, how would a young woman know that? And Köse, she's not lived here long enough!"

"Maybe the internet."

"You have half an hour to find information about the

links between FSS and that building using the same info they would have and the net. You're assuming they knew of its existence unless it was found purely by chance. A pint is yours if you produce the evidence." He looked at his watch. "Your time begins now, start surfing, if that's the correct term." Cyril pointed to a computer station. "You can ask for help from your colleagues here if you struggle. I need to talk to Julie."

***

Shaw watched as she put the key in the lock and opened the door. He noticed the cat flap and then the cat sitting on the table next to a polystyrene box.

"Dr Shaw, meet Tommy. Tommy this is Callum. Be nice to him, at least at first. He can be funny – beautiful but unpredictable."

"Do you mean me or the cat?"

The cat stood and stretched. His back arched beautifully before walking with a nonchalant air that only cats exhibit as he moved toward the corner of the table nearest to Shaw.

"You are rather beautiful, Tommy. You can sense I like cats and I'm kind." He slid his hand onto the cat's head and ran his fingers over his ears and then down his back. The arch appeared again as the cat turned. The purring, a deep internal rattle, grew in volume. "You know you're beautiful and I know you could tolerate this for hours. You too are gentle and kind."

"He'll have you his slave if you're willing and he's definitely male and unpredict ..." She did not finish the sentence as Shaw withdrew his hand as Tommy turned biting his little finger. He nudged the cat away as he gave a yelp. "Fuck! The sodding thing's just bitten me. He's drawn blood for fuck's sake."

Tommy jumped from the table and shot through the cat flap. Shaw went to the sink and turned on the tap. Both watched as the diluted blood swirled in fine lines on the white porcelain before flowing down the plughole.

"Keep it there. I have some TCP in the bathroom and a plaster. The trouble with cat bites – you don't know the last thing he killed and ate but I bet he's licking his arse end now to take your flavour away." She giggled and left the room.

Shaw kept his finger beneath the running water whilst glancing through the faded net curtains into the yard. He focused on the yellow combine stored under the Dutch barn. His car was where he had left it but was covered with what looked like a tarpaulin. Movement to his left caused him to lean further forward. His heart beat quickly as he turned off the tap and looked at the door.

"I found it. Sit and the nurse will attend the mauled digit."

Shaw pointed to the window. "Is there someone else here?"

***

Julie was not in her office but he was ushered in. There was a sweet smell that grew stronger as he moved towards her desk. As always it was immaculate. On the corner stood a diffuser, the black spills spread into what looked like a broken fan. He bent and immediately the strength of the smell was enriched. He read the label – *Oud*. He had never heard of it. Whilst on his feet he took the opportunity to study the specimens stored within the various jars or trapped in resin. He did not touch them but he ran his finger along the shelf checking for dust. There was none. The one jar that always seemed to attract him was not there. In some ways, he was relieved. He settled in the chair and listened to the music playing on the radio. A piece by Bruch, the violin concerto, broke his train of thought and he stared at the small radio before closing his eyes. A memory of his mother came immediately to mind, her body swaying as the bow moved as if in unison. He thought of her kindness, the selfless sacrifice she had made those many years ago when he was a child. It was, he felt, her courage and strong moral guidance that had shaped him. His father, although flawed, had always wanted the best for him and it took a while before he had realised that.

He was totally entranced in his thoughts when Julie entered.

"I was told you were lurking, Bennett ..." She heard the music and immediately knew just where he was. He opened his eyes and stood.

"Sorry, miles away."

"Years away but understandable." Moving to him she kissed him tenderly and switched off the radio.

"As public servants, some of us have work to do," she smiled. "Have you had coffee?"

"Thanks, but no. Bernard Jones has turned up but unfortunately, he's dead. All the indicators suggest suicide but ..."

"I've heard. White has the task you'll be pleased to know." She added a pod into the coffee machine and pointed to the cups. "Are you sure?"

"Yes, thank you, positive. The silicone mask and hands. Can we check the scale and accuracy before we do anything else? Without those and no further forensic investigation to the contrary, I'd have written it off as suicide. The poor bugger had a good deal to contend with in his life and I've experienced people do it for less."

"Murder?" Julie sat down. The smell of the coffee drifted towards Cyril.

"Or assisted suicide. The clues from the location have brought retribution clearly to the front of our investigation. The whereabouts of his daughter are still unknown as are those of the young woman who could have sculpted the body parts. As well as the smell of coffee and the delightful smell of Oud, I can't get the stronger smell of foul play out of my nostrils, Julie. It's a copper thing."

"Owen will be attending the autopsy, I take it?" She looked up failing to hide her smile.

"Without a shadow of doubt. What the hell is Oud?" He pointed to the diffuser.

"Oud, Cyril, it's pronounced 'ood'. It's one of the most desirable and expensive perfume ingredients in the world. It comes from the bark of the Agar tree. Before you deliberately yawn, you'll enjoy this fact, Cyril, it appeals to me. It's created when the bark is infected by a parasitic mould and the tree fights that creating a precious, dark and fragrant resin. Only two percent of the trees are infected and produce it."

"Right. Here endeth the lesson. Sorry I asked."

"How does £5,000 per pound grab you?"

"I'm in the wrong job."

She took a file from her desk. "I'll keep you posted about Jones. Let me have the mask and hands."

Cyril stood and moved towards the door before pointing to the gap on the shelf.

"Another lecture visual aid?"

"Mind your own business. See you tonight."

Chapter 20

Shaw sat at the table and held his hand steady as the TCP was applied.

"You often get farm staff popping in for bits and bobs. The barns belong to them. It's reassuring to be honest. More eyes on the place. You can never be sure who's about. Farm theft is a major issue but this farm is well off a main road if you can call the country lanes main."

She applied the plaster and washed her hands.

"Let's hope you haven't given Tommy some disease, I'd never forgive you. He'll not go near while you smell of TCP that's for sure so you're safe and so is he."

As if on cue Tommy came through the cat flap and moved to his food bowl. Shaw watched trying to forgive him but moved away.

"I'm sure the person in the yard was a woman, a young woman. For a minute I thought ..." He stopped himself. "My car's been covered. Have you done it?"

"They're spraying in the barn and suggested it be covered to protect the paintwork."

Shaw frowned. "Why spray?"

"We get all sorts of vermin here, two legged as well as

four," she winked at him. "I'll show the injured soldier my room, the bedroom, if he's not suffering too much pain and then I have something I want you to see." Her smile said everything and he felt his face flush.

Shaw stood. The thought of his hand, the courtyard visitor and his car were all quickly forgotten and he followed as if led by the nose.

***

Dr Peter White held the silicone mask next to Bernard Jones's head which was positioned for the exercise on a head block. His clothing had been removed for further forensic investigation. A number of photographs were taken and Owen could immediately see them on the screen from where he stood.

"The likeness is very good but this was clearly not moulded from the real thing. The face is a tad smaller and the hands also bigger. You'll notice Jones has a mallet finger on the left hand and this gives the digit a crooked appearance." He lifted the hand and pointed to the deformity. "There is damage to the forehead above the eye. Looking at the contusion I'd say that happened pre-death, two maybe three days ago. There would have been much swelling and maybe closure to the eye. We'll look in more detail but blunt impact trauma. It's all in the looking, Owen."

"Right!" Owen held back a yawn. At least now they had confirmation about the head and the hands.

"Autopsy derives from the Greek word autopsia, Owen, to see with one's own eyes. It can make all the difference as you can clearly witness."

"DCI Bennett always says 'If you stare long enough, the clues are there for you to see', and I guess that's often confirmed in your job. Do we have a time of death?"

White looked up, his face slightly distorted by the Perspex convex face guard. "The general appearance of his overall complexion is that of cherry-red showing CO intoxication brought about by the inhalation of the vehicle's exhaust and oxygen deprivation. It's the binding of carbon monoxide to haemoglobin so the blood cannot transport oxygen. It gives him a healthy appearance don't you think?"

Owen found the comment strange considering the person's situation. "For a dead man I suppose it does."

"You'll also see this cherry-red in the viscera when we open the chest cavity. I'll use the Virchow technique, are you familiar with that?"

"I believe it means removal of the organs one at a time?" Owen smiled remembering a similar conversation he'd had with Dr Julie Pritchett when he first started to attend post-mortems.

"Very good. The time, you asked. We know from the medic at the scene that rigor mortis was showing and that could indicate anything from two to six hours after death depending on temperature. However, the muscles are now relaxing which suggests to me he had been dead about six hours before he was discovered. Now that's intriguing. What we know is that he was found around 7am if the report is accurate."

They both looked at the clock on the wall.

"Let's say eight hours since that point. I feel he's been dead longer than we originally thought as we see a fixation of the liver mortis. More importantly, there's evidence of

Tardieu spots, also known as petechiae. We see that decomposition is fast approaching. He could have died the day before but I'm speculating. When I open the stomach and view the contents, we'll have a better idea."

"The van was not in the carpark at 11pm according to a reliable witness. It was first seen just before 7am so we have a broad time window. Could the body have been moved?"

"There's evidence the arm has been moved either involuntarily or deliberately and forensic assessment will give a direction on that. There's some staining, livor mortis, to one side but then greater signs on the other. It suggests the person may well have died in the van somewhere else and been driven to the location where they were found later." White looked up and shrugged his shoulders. "Our science only permits a degree of vision into the past at this early stage. You and your colleagues must use what we find here and look … what is the saying? If you look long enough etc. Let's both do that. I think there's more to this case than just someone reaching life's tipping point."

***

The bed was empty when he woke. The very early morning travel, the excitement and the sex had induced sleep. Checking his watch, he believed he had been asleep for about an hour. Where she had lain was now cool but the smell of her perfume lingered on the pillow. He could also smell the aftermath of their sex. He lay back with his eyes closed and folded his hands behind his head, trying to recall the time he had first seen her. It came to his mind quickly and brought with it a smile. He could see it clearly. He had been driving back to Leeds, it was late afternoon, the country road was awash and there she was hitching a lift, drenched and desperate. A true damsel in distress. It had seemed so easy. He could hear her voice even now.

"Thanks for stopping. Sorry, I'm wetting your lovely seats, sorry." She had opened the rear door and tossed in the rucksack that seemed bigger than her. She had sounded so young and innocent. Remembering her next words made him openly chuckle.

"It's pissing and shitting it down and I'm soaked through to my knickers."

The windows of the car, he remembered, began to steam up and he had put on the heater to clear the windscreen.

"There's a travel rug on the back seat beneath your luggage. Wrap it around you before you catch your death."

It was as if it were only yesterday. His mind rushed on, his flat, her in the shower for what seemed like an age, the meal he had prepared which she had eaten hungrily, a few snatched words but she had said nothing that first night, not even *thank you*. The spare room became hers. She would sit all day and read, oblivious of time and days as if lost in her own world. She would get angry if her hair was touched or any tenderness or kindness displayed towards her. It was as though she had thrown up an emotional barrier but then at other times, she became a different girl.

The day's sunlight penetrating the lace curtains appeared like fine needles, defused and milky white but pin straight, capturing the floating minutiae that seemed to dance as if energised by the sun's warmth. It was a distraction taking him a few moments to bring the whole room into clear focus. Seeing the cat curled at the foot of the bed watching him, its tail moving like a slow metronome brought an immediate reaction and he tucked his feet up and away before grabbing the pillow and placing it before him like a shield. Tommy yawned showing needle-like teeth before standing, stretching and plucking at the blanket on which he stood. Within seconds the cat leaped from the bed, a dull thud was heard as it hit the floor and scampered from the room. Callum Shaw breathed a sigh of relief as he looked at the plaster on his hand and remembered the creature's capricious nature.

The house was silent. There was nothing, not even the sound of birds. Throwing the quilt away he slid from the bed, slipped on boxers and trousers before grabbing his sweater. The bare boards felt rough once he moved from the bedside rug. Looking round the room, having been too preoccupied the previous evening, he could see the amount of neglect she had described and yet there was an innocence in the way the place was furnished. The wardrobe, dressing table, stool and chairs were obviously pre-owned but they were clean and ordered. The walls, however, showed signs of damp and in two or three places the paper curled away at the upper corners.

The floor boards protested as he moved to the door. At the top of the stairs, he listened, the sound of voices was muffled and almost lost and then they were replaced by music. It was the radio. He relaxed. There was no one in the kitchen. A mug and breakfast bowl were on the table alongside a box of cereal and a carton of milk that contradicted the time of day. The stone flags felt cold beneath his bare feet. Moving back to the stairs he looked down the corridor to the left. His curiosity got the better of him. *Remember what curiosity did to the cat!* The thought brought a smile. He stopped at a door to his left, the stairs to his right. It was closed. He knocked but there was no response. He listened and looked back towards the kitchen. Nothing could be heard other than the drone of the radio.

"Hello. Anyone in the land of the living in here today?" He laughed as if to calm his own insecurity. He looked at the over-painted metal, lever handle, typical of a cottage and pushed down. The click sounded louder than expected. He entered. The light filtered from one small window in the far wall but not enough to illuminate the area. His hand instinctively searched the wall to his left for a light switch. He was rewarded and within seconds the bulb suspended from one of the wooden beams lit the room. He stopped in his tracks.

***

The stomach was weighed before the contents were viewed. White turned to Owen after he had placed them in a large stainless steel bowl. "Never the prettiest of sights, Detective Inspector, nor is it the best aroma in the world but an essential tool for calculating the time of death, providing we believe this was a meal eaten just prior to death. If it was consumed a day or two before it's as useful as a broken clock."

Owen checked his own watch and then looked back at the procedure.

"It's not easy to determine what was eaten but peas can

often be seen, skins from tomatoes and seeds are also common but there's none here. From what I can make out at a guess, there's about thirty-four percent of the last meal consumed still present so I would suggest between eight and ten hours from the time of death. We can do further tests. This assessment of the last meal taken is another indicator. So, what we are seeing is the person could have died in the carpark but other evidence suggests he may have been moved after death." He looked up towards Owen. "I'm aware we have contradictory evidence at the moment but with more scrutiny we can narrow that down. I believe it was wise to call this one suspicious as it's certainly not straightforward."

***

Shaw stared at the walls to either side of the window. Wide wooden battens had been attached horizontally to the rough plaster walls and set at two heights, the upper line at about two metres, adult eye level. The contents of each wall seemed disparate. Stapled to the wood appeared a selection of photographs. Beneath each was an old table. He moved to the right and inspected the display. The first thing to attract his attention was a clay head. It stared across the room to the other wall. Its detail was finely sculpted and he knew he had seen something similar before. The hands placed to either side were well crafted. Turning one in his hand, its life-like qualities made him think of Gülen Köse. Like the other two pieces of clay, they had been fired to bisque but also coated with a clear finish. The head was without hair and whoever had carved the clay had concentrated purely on the face. It was hollow and holes were punctured in the back of the head as a prevention of cracking during firing.

The photographs were a mixed collection. A number showed a child and then there were others of adults and a family unit, two adults and a girl. Some were clearly older than others. A close up of the male shown from many angles made Shaw stop. It was a perfect match for the clay sculpture. The meeting with the detective at the university came immediately to mind and at the same time a shiver ran down his neck. Suddenly the room seemed cold and even more hostile. There were then news cuttings with the headline 'Missing'. He read the article detailing Kerry Jones's disappearance, it seemed relatively topical, the news cutting clean. He stared at the photograph central to the article. The face he knew stared back, the face of the young woman he had given the lift to; the girl who always wanted to be called Sarah, she had said it was not her real name but she had her reasons, the same woman who had taken him to bed that morning. Positioned next to her photograph was that of a man.

"What the hell is this shrine all about?" His words were floated into the silence.

Searching the news article, he could find no date. Stapled beneath it, however, were three other news cuttings. Bernard Jones was missing. Reference was briefly made of Kerry's past disappearance. The photograph was clear and he compared it to the ceramic head. There was clearly a match.

Shaw unpicked the staples releasing one photograph from the batten, the largest photograph present. It was of

Kerry with her father. She was dressed in what appeared to be a prom outfit, a long and elegant gown showing off the young woman's figure. Everything about her was beautiful – her hair, makeup and yet there was something about the awkwardness of their pose, her father's face, his expression. Shaw dwelled momentarily on his features. He knew that look and he suddenly felt nauseous and a blistering sense of guilt.

It took a few moments for him to move to the other wall just to gain a moment's clarity. Here there were more photographs but also cuttings from magazines, snapshots of buildings and the countryside. They seemed out of place and in total contrast to the opposite wall. Studying them carefully, he realised they concealed other pictures beneath them. His hand shook slightly as he unpicked the lower staples of the first, before lifting the upper photograph. The revelation made his heart skip. Facing him was a picture of himself. He was on the bed, naked. Leaning forward he looked more intently. It was taken in his Leeds flat, the painting above the bed was so familiar. He looked as though he were asleep. *When was this?* His mind raced. He knew who had taken it. Moving to the next cutting, he observed an image of the obelisk in Ripon Market Square, with hesitancy he did the same. Lifting it he saw another shot, this time he was with 'Sarah'. Their horrified expressions told the full story of their compromise. He knew the place. It was his office, his university private work space. "Shit!" Snatching the image from the wall he tore it into small pieces before tossing them onto the table below. "What the fuck is going on here?"

He had seen enough, the other four pictures would

remain covered for the time being at least.

As he moved to leave the room, he flicked off the light switch and closed the door.

"Fucking rude to snoop. Did I ever do that at your place?"

"Christ, you bloody well startled me. How long have you been there Sarah or should I now call you Kerry?"

She stood blocking his way, a hammer in one hand and a large kitchen knife in the other. Tommy stood a few paces behind her and then moved between her feet.

He calmed. "Sorry, you'd gone. I must have dropped off for a bit. I came down when I heard the radio. I was looking for you. I thought you'd be in the kitchen."

"Open the door and go back in but put on the light as you go. There's a chair by the window. Sit on it and don't say another fucking word."

Shaw backed in following her instructions. Finding the chair, he sat. His eyes flashed to the display of photographs and cuttings.

She perched on the table. "What you see here, is my life pitiful as it is. Did you have a good upbringing, a warm and caring family who nurtured and loved you?" She paused looking into his eyes.

He nodded.

"I take it you were spoiled, given every opportunity to be a freethinking young man guided to develop a strong, personal moral compass, a compass that was built from example, kindness, love and caring?"

"Yes." Shaw trapped his hands between his knees and looked at the wall containing his photograph and the confetti detritus scattered on the table opposite, realising the contradiction.

"When I was very young, I too thought I was loved. I did love, I loved my parents deeply. I loved my dad, I was his special girl, his Cinderella but I couldn't pronounce that word I said 'Drella'. It would make him laugh and hold me. It was our special secret." She paused biting her lip but gripping the knife vertically and stabbing the point into the table.

"That's lovely."

"No, it wasn't. I didn't know then but he was grooming me. He bathed me as mum worked long shifts, sometimes she stayed over at work owing to things happening and they needed her there but I needed her too. He washed me intimately, inappropriately I learned later, but then it seemed so normal as he was my dad and he'd do nothing to harm me, would he? Fathers in fairy tales didn't do that. I didn't realise the reason at the time. He would also get into the bath. I had dolls in the bath but he wanted me to play with him. You know what that meant?"

Shaw nodded but made no reply.

"I loved him, the man who called me his Cinderella, we had our own secrets that nobody else should know about. They were ours and ours alone. I was very confused and I'd do whatever he asked. He asked me to perform sex acts on him and that became a regular thing. When I was maybe twelve, he raped me. I was so confused."

Shaw noticed the tone of her voice change as she started to sob.

"He'd often ask to see me naked and comment on my changing body. In a way it was flattering because he used words that caressed my ego, my emotional, immature consciousness. I knew it to be wrong but didn't want to say anything to mum, I didn't want to break up the family. He said if I were to tell anyone, just like Cinderella, I'd no longer be beautiful nor loved, not by him or by mum and if my friends heard they'd never speak to me again." Kerry tore the photograph of her in the prom gown from the wall. "Cinderella was going to the ball. It was then I told him, just after that photograph was taken. I knew what he wanted and suddenly for some reason … maybe it was seeing mum shagging that other bloke, seeing that my family was just a sham, a cesspit of lies and false promises. I'd loved them both and within a moment my world was shattered and in pieces and I was still a kid. It was that day I made up my mind to run away when the opportunity was right for me and never to return. I also vowed one day I'd confront him, tell the world. He'd stopped doing things to me but I know he was grooming others. I thought I lived in a world of kindness and all along I lived in a shithole of depravity. And then when I left, I met …"

Shaw deliberately interrupted knowing what she was about to say. "He's missing, you know that, I've seen you have the news cuttings." He pointed to the wall.

"He is, he was but he's not now."

She pulled the blade from the table, collected the hammer and with all the venom she could muster, brought it down hard onto the ceramic head of her father. It exploded sending myriad pieces over the table and floor. Shaw leaned back in the chair and Tommy, who had been on the far table, shot from the room.

"As I said, he'll not be missing for much longer." She pointed the knife at him. "I need you to sit there a little longer. I'll only be a minute." She placed the hammer by the shattered pottery.

Chapter 21

The first hours of the morning seemed to evaporate, mainly dealing with the paperwork that came with the job alongside the many calls and interruptions.

Cyril stared at the tea cosy knitted in the shape of a black sheep. It stared back at him through two button eyes. It had arrived on his desk that morning, a gift from a lady in control. Getting Owen to bring a simple cup and saucer had been a challenge, to train him to bring a teapot covered with a sheep might be a step too far. There was a distraction from that dilemma as his mobile sat in front of it on speaker.

"Forensics have some news regarding the van. As it was stolen there's quite a lot of conflicting DNA traces but I'm assured the last person to drive it was Bernard Jones. Touch analysis shows his DNA on the door handle, the steering wheel and gear lever. It was even on the plastic end of the hose that hung into the car. His jacket was used to block the partially open window that held the hose. None of the other prominent lifted prints have shown up on the national database but they're checking two other strong DNA traces from the passenger area."

Cyril thought for a moment. "Anything from the mattress,

Brian?"

"Yes, loads and most of it of no importance. It's had a life that mattress and has been the home to a variety of wildlife. They believe its final few years were spent under cover but open to the elements. I'm informed the Forensic Entomologist is taking a closer look. DNA covered but it also has traces of paint, food, rat and mouse shit and of course, vomit."

"If he drove to the carpark then that contradicts some of the autopsy's findings as far as timing is concerned. As one door opens another will shut with a bang. Thanks, to think I should have been off today. The life of a jolly copper!"

He had even arranged to meet Julie for lunch at the Harrogate Tea Rooms. He still might manage it if things did not get too frenetic.

***

Kerry lifted the latch and kicked open the door as she bent to pick up the polystyrene box she had popped on the floor. Shaw was still on the chair. She moved within two metres of him and placed the box on the stone flags before bending, kissing his head and then moving to the opposite table. The knife was still in her hand. That sensitive gesture seemed to contradict everything he was experiencing.

"Thank you for doing as I asked." She fixed him with a stare until his feelings swung the other way and he felt uncomfortable again.

"I'm sorry. I had no idea about your father. If I had …"

Kerry held up her hand signalling for him to stop.

"You'd not have taken advantage of me, not abused me

either? You knew all along. Men like you see our vulnerability."

"It wasn't like that. I didn't force you. You could've left at any time, walked away. You, Sarah, decided to stay. If anything, being there was cathartic for you, it helped you discover who you really were and what you wanted to do with your life. How long had you been missing from home?"

"Call me Kerry, Sarah's gone, I no longer need to hide behind her, not now. Long enough to know I needed some kind of respite, some kind of home and for that I knew there'd be a cost. Did you really think a girl of my age would want to be regularly mauled by you unless it was in exchange for a place of safety, for money in my pocket? I'd hoped you'd be decent and honourable. How I allowed myself to make that mistake so often I'll never understand. Näively, I tried to believe you cared."

"I did. I know that sounds feeble now but it's the truth." His voice was almost a whisper.

"Often?"

"Young women in my position have to survive. Did you care? Why do I seek real affection, someone to care for me, cherish me? I began to believe that I must always be Cinders and never Cinderella. I soon realised I was a convenient toy. Maybe it was all my fault from the very beginning."

Shaw looked at the torn photograph and watched as she collected a few pieces before letting them fall from her fingers. She moved back and perched on the other table.

"These memories are like sand through an hour glass, and just like time, we move on. I moved on. I left you and found someone who really cared, someone who showed true compassion, someone who didn't abuse my weakness. I then heard that you'd left, run to another part of the country before anyone spoke out and the shit hit the fan. You're cruel, you're a groomer of the vulnerable and an abuser. To find I had one in my short life is tough but to realise I had many and then you is more than fucking careless, it's life changing." She laughed but then stopped as the reality of the words hit home and she began to weep. Soon she recovered her composure.

Pointing the tip of the knife at the box. "It's for you. What's in there is yours."

Shaw looked down and then back at her, his apprehension clear in his expression.

"Let's say it's a gift from an admirer. You can open it if you wish."

Shaw brought his hands to his mouth and he breathed onto them feeling the instant warmth.

"Now! Open it!" The firmness and volume of the order belied her size.

***

Cyril sat with Owen as they watched the news report of the discovery of the body at the location. The covered trailer containing the van could be seen leaving the site as the reporter spoke to camera.

"The Police are interested in speaking to anyone who was in the vicinity between 6pm yesterday and 9am today and they would be grateful for any dashcam footage if you were near Fountains Abbey between those times. They would also like to speak to anyone in the area who might have seen the vehicle." The camera panned to the covered trailer as he began to describe the van. The police contact number flashed onto the screen.

"It was still wearing its legit plates when found and there's no ANPR in the area. It hasn't been registered in Harrogate nor Ripon so I'm assuming it was either moved with cloned plates or it's been stored locally until needed." Cyril doodled on the note pad as he spoke.

"If it were driven at night either by Jones or someone else, there's little chance of it being picked up," Owen surmised. "If it were Jones, where's he been? Would it be worth doing a sweep of the properties within a set radius of the scene?"

"Are you aware of the cost implication of that little exercise, Owen, and how would we justify that if the guy has in fact committed suicide? The hammer of bloody Thor would descend on our heads, actually on my head for wasting valuable resources at a time when every penny counts. Wherever he's been hiding is, I feel, irrelevant at this stage but might become significant the more we know. What we need is more information from our friends in Forensics, that's what we need not a bloody extensive search."

***

Shaw leaned forward. Kerry could almost feel his reluctance. Before he lifted the lid, he looked at her. There was a clear anxiety in his face.

"I've not put your nemesis in there, it's not Tommy waiting to finish you off."

The polystyrene squeaked as the tight-fitting lid's lip left the box. He looked inside and then back at Kerry, a frown clearly visible on his brow.

She nodded. "Go on, remove it. It'll not bite you."

Both hands entered the box and the clay head was extracted. He stared at the brown bisque sculpture. He was looking at himself. He felt cold and a numbness seemed to grip him.

"I … I don't understand? You didn't make this."

"You weren't listening. An admirer made it. Good isn't it. The likeness is amazing. I thought about that as I looked at you when you were grunting on top of me earlier."

Shaw lifted his head and looked at the ceiling. "I'm sorry, truly sorry. I'd no idea. I thought …"

"Shhh!" She placed the knife blade to her lips as if it were a finger. "You know what thought did? I understand, I really do. Daddy said the same when he sat in that very chair. As a child, I loved Harry Potter, in particular Dumbledore, it was an escape into another world for me." She laughed gently. "The head you're holding is hollow. I put it to my ear like a shell but instead of hearing crashing waves or the lapping of the sea, I can hear Dumbledore whisper: 'If you listen carefully enough, the past whispers to you.' Try it, or are you frightened of the past?"

***

"Bennett." Cyril moved to his desk, his mobile firmly planted to his ear. "When? Where? Parliament Street, the Turkish baths? Do we know who it is, who it depicts? I want Forensics there before it's moved. I'm on my way. Get photographs uplifted now."

Shakti was the first officer he saw in the room and he addressed her as he passed her desk. "Pictures will be coming in of another silicone face that's been found. I want them on the whiteboards pronto and anyone involved in the case needs to see them. I need to know who it is. We know what happened to the last person who shared a resemblance. Please spread the word. Anything, and I mean anything." He paused. "Also try checking for any CCTV coverage of the Turkish baths on Parliament Street, there may be private ones too on the restaurants and bars in the vicinity. Let me know as soon as." He held up his phone as he disappeared through the door.

The traffic seemed slower than usual. Temporary lights at the junction of Panel Ash Road seemed to stretch the cars in front for some distance. Annoyingly he had seen the chaos earlier in the day on his way to the station and should have planned a better route. Within fifteen minutes he turned down West Park. The ginnel to Robert Street to his right made him wish for home. Again, the traffic built as he approached the Cenotaph but at least the one-way system was only held by the lights and the bottom of Parliament Street where two lanes became three. He would not travel that far. Cyril pulled in to the spare parking spot just before the Winter Gardens.

Two officers stood together further down the hill and he assumed correctly they were protecting the face that was hooked onto the fence directly in front of the building from passing pedestrians. An elderly couple stood nearby.

Bennett flashed his ID even though he had been recognised by one of the officers. They separated giving

Cyril a glance at the object. He crouched and stared at the ghoulish mask and, as with the previous one, he was impressed by the detail.

"Sir, Mr and Mrs Eagin, they called about the face. They stopped two school kids from taking it. They remembered reading in *The Advertiser* about similar items being found."

Cyril turned and spoke to the couple. "Thank you for your trouble and your time."

"It wasn't there where it is now, it was a bit further up the railing. We were coming across the road and I saw them, two lads, remove something. I thought they might be destroying the flowers planted in the troughs but then one put the object to his face and it immediately brought the article to mind. I just thought it could belong to the baths. I shouted and they stopped. I told them the police were on their way and I had their photographs should they run away with it. I showed them my phone and I held out my hand. I was honestly expecting expletives but they just passed it to me with an apology. I hung it on the fence and called." He looked at his wife who had been nodding throughout his narration.

"Thank you, your action today has been vital to an ongoing investigation. I'll need your address and details and we'll be in touch. I don't need to delay you further. I'm grateful to you both."

The couple smiled at each other and then at Cyril. "I'm relieved. One never knows if one is doing the correct thing these days especially when tackling today's youth."

As he turned, Cyril noticed the tell-tale sign of a CCTV camera on the gable end of the entrance to the Winter Gardens. He called control to request they check the morning's footage. If it was recorded he would examine it.

***

Shakti had pinned the images onto the board and contacted all who had been directly involved in the case. Stuart Park came into the Incident Room after receiving the call.

"Is that the mask, Shak?" He moved closer and inspected it.

"Found outside the Turkish baths. Hanging on the fence."

"It's Dr Callum Shaw. He was Gülen Köse's personal tutor until he moved away. The details are here." He checked the boards and tapped the relevant notes he had made of the missing university student. "She's Turkish." He paused and turned to Shakti. "Turkish and missing and this was hanging outside the Turkish baths? It's telling us all we need to know."

He went to a computer screen and within minutes the staff photograph linked to his university website appeared.

"They're not all on but his is. It's here." He copied and printed the image.

"That's the man." Shakti picked up her phone and relayed the details to Cyril.

"CSI has arrived. I want as many people in for a briefing within the hour. If they're off try to get them here." He looked at his watch, shook his wrist and looked again. In one hour." He hung up and immediately dialled Julie to cancel their lunch date.

Chapter 22

Shaw nursed the ceramic head on his lap for some time. The silence hung thickly as if no words could penetrate. Suddenly the mood was broken.

"He sat here, your father?"

"He held his own clay head, just as you're doing now. How do we forgive, Callum? What makes us turn the other cheek and put the hurt behind us? Daddy knew."

Hearing the word Daddy brought a chill to his arms and his neck. For a moment she was a child again, she displayed a weakness and vulnerability but he did not take advantage. There was a long pause as he looked at the ceramic face before focusing on Kerry's question. As he spoke, he deliberately made his voice shaky and his answer sound uncertain. "Forgive us our sins as we forgive those who have sinned against us."

Kerry sighed. "How long have you known that?"

"Since I was a child. Did you learn it as a kid?"

"Since I was a child." She wanted to mimic his voice but thought it cruel. "I forgive you if you forgive me. Is that like an eye for an eye or am I being … childish?"

Her word childish hit him like a slap. He had

underestimated the young woman.

"In that deal what are you forgiving, Callum Shaw?"

"This, the duplicity. This is not what you said it would be. I don't see a judge or a jury but I feel as though I'm on trial. Was your father on trial too? If so, Kerry, what was your verdict?"

She did not expect this response, she believed he would be bowed and beaten but he seemed to rally. Had he seen something in her, maybe it was a moment of innocence, doubt or fear? Had he seen through her? Had she pushed him too far into a corner? She took a deep breath to re-establish some control, a need inculcated by her sudden uncertainty.

"When my father sat there, in that very seat where you are now, he said he was sorry, he was contrite. I learned that word when I was planning to confront him and I said to myself, if there's contrition, if there's genuine remorse, then there's hope of forgiveness, hope that I might have a family again and if there's forgiveness there should be trust, do you not agree?"

Shaw frowned trying to comprehend words that were coming from the mouth of someone he saw as young, someone he thought he knew. The confusion made him feel as though he were in a bizarre play, a farce. He wanted to call out *Oh no you didn't* but something made him hold back just in case it was not all some kind of huge joke, a laugh? He looked across again at the wall and the realisation struck him hard – it was far from a joke.

"Are you a family again, Kerry?"

She side-stepped the question as if it would interrupt her script. "Forgiveness brings trust. Do you trust me?"

Shaw looked perplexed. “What do you mean, trust?”

“For me to forgive, I must trust you and you, Callum, must trust me. Daddy did.”

Shaw nodded. *Anything to stop this foolish charade*, came to his mind. He had had enough. “I trust you.” The words were flat conveying little sincerity.

“You must get on your knees and look at my feet and ask for my forgiveness. That’s all you have to do but you must say it as if you mean it.” She looked at him knowing what he was thinking. Funny, with trust came that tingle of uncertainty or was it fear? “You can walk out if you wish. There are no locks just the words you said earlier. ‘I love you, Kerry.’ You know that don’t you? Remember those words? When was it, just a few hours ago?”

“I do. You know I do.”

“But you’re also an abuser of the weak and frail. You know that too. You must just go but if you do, you must know that I’ll telephone the police and tell them all I know. They will then inform the university; you will be interviewed and others may talk about their experiences with you too. You know the probable outcome of that. You choose.”

Shaw put the ceramic head back in the box before kneeling, all the while looking at her, uncertainty clearly written across his face.

“What do you say, Callum Shaw?”

“I’m sorry, Kerry.” He lowered his head to look at the floor. “Please, please forgive me.”

Moving quickly, she collected the hammer and with one sweeping upward motion she struck him just above the right eye with all the force she could muster. The sound, a dull thud, seemed to die away immediately, lost in the moment as blood gushed from the inflicted wound. Shaw slumped onto the box and then fell sideways.

"You're forgiven." Kerry stared down at the prostrate figure. "I trusted you when I got in your car, you assured me you would help me. It's so hard to trust again."

***

Cyril came into the Incident Room and checked the photographs on the whiteboards. The silicone face he had just seen was definitely that of Dr Callum Shaw. He proceeded to the briefing. Owen, April, Shakti and Stuart Park were already present.

"Is this it?" Cyril looked, nodding at the congregation and then down at the folder as it was slid in front of him. He flicked through the pages noting the headings and the photographs within each section. "Stuart, remind us about your conversation with Callum Shaw."

Stuart Park went through his notes.

"I recall you had a gut feeling about him and the student, Köse."

"I really wasn't sure. I think I told you Shaw could well have been having an affair with her but I also said he was extremely professional and outwardly plausible. Evidence suggested he seemed to care about the girl and maybe even more about the standard of her work. He demonstrated genuine concern when he saw her disappointing later works. I spoke with a boyfriend she'd been seeing," he checked his notes, "Derek Coulson. He was also concerned about her, again her complete change of personality and he seemed to lay that at Shaw's door, the fact he left. It was from that point he said she changed. As if she were only secure when he was there."

"We'll come back to him but let's concentrate on the tutor particularly his meetings with her after he left. How did he explain those?"

"Again, purely professional. I made enquiries and it seems it's not uncommon for some tutors or mentors to keep in touch with students once they qualify and leave. It's a two-way process. Some have an affinity that goes beyond the limits of the course."

"Let's remember she was in university accommodation for the first two years and in her final year she moved into a private rental. She never went into arrears. We also have to remember she met and worked with Bernard Jones, left because of the alleged inappropriate sexual advances." Cyril held open the file.

"So, is he responsible for both his daughter and her disappearance? Has he killed them both and then himself?" Shakti asked.

"If he's responsible, why have we received the clues, the devious clues that led us in a certain direction. Both men are linked in different ways to Gülen Köse. She was skilled enough to create the body parts, she knew Harrogate but just how well did she know Bernard Jones?"

"Where was she living after university? She shouldn't have even been here owing to her visa expiry. Leeds? Harrogate? In a hole?" Cyril flicked through the folder before standing and dragging up a flip chart near to the group. "Let's remember the first clues, the body parts came in one at a time. Each relevant. Some thought it was a cry for help, abuse of either a physical, psychological or sexual nature. It was assumed that maybe justice was not delivered. If it's linked to Köse, why wasn't Shaw targeted first? She was with him for a year and knew him for longer? That length of time meant he had a greater impact on her life than Jones."

"Jones was the latest perpetrator, he meant nothing to her. They weren't academic equals?" Park added but did not sound convinced by his own theory.

April stood and took the pen from Cyril. "We're working on assumptions and not evidence. We're assuming Köse made the props. Not a fact. We're presuming Shaw was having an affair with the same young woman." She looked at Park who shook his head.

"Not a fact."

"There's no evidence to suggest any impropriety between Bernard Jones and Köse. So, what facts do we actually have?" April looked at Cyril.

"Shaw still works at the university. Fact. Both women are still missing. Fact. Jones is dead in suspicious circumstances. To be established." Park responded swiftly.

Cyril turned to Park. "Go over, you've been to see him previously, don't call him as if he's a wrong 'un, he'll flit. Find him, interview him. We have his address from the background check you ran. If he's gone walkabout check his place. Talk to neighbours and colleagues. I'll organise the neighbouring force's full co-operation and a warrant although with two missing young women who might be in danger that will not be difficult. April, his car, his phone, his bank, anything. See where he's travelled in the last two weeks. Check ANPR. It might take a while but do whatever it takes. Shakti, get his photograph ready to go out there.

Liaise with Stuart. If he's not where he should be I want it posted."

***

Kerry sat at the kitchen table. The unused bowl, spoon and cereal packet were still there but now there was also a plastic freezer bag containing a computer USB pen drive and a laptop. The cover, covered in a variety of stickers, was positioned before her. Tommy was curled on the cushion on her lap. Placing the drive into the socket she clicked on the first file. A collection of photographs appeared, close-up, candid images of both Jones and Shaw taken at a number of angles and appearing like small tiles. She added many of the photographs stored on the laptop to the file, most had been displayed and pinned to the battens in the other room along with others she had on a private file. The last element to be added was the edited recording made of Jones made in the same room, the confessional, the admission of guilt. It was only his answers and never the questions or conversation. She listened briefly to check the quality and clarity:

"I don't know why I started to touch her. I loved her and she loved me. She was my Cinderella. She was young and she couldn't say the word, she used to say Drella …" Kerry moved the recording forward and stopped it at a point she had memorised:

"I just went to her room. I knew she'd just had a bath …" Kerry moved it on again a short distance. "I was so sorry. I couldn't believe that I had just raped my daughter, my Cinderella."

The words never got any easier to hear, the memories still resounded. She swallowed and focused on the task in hand. Shaw's confession would be added later. She saved what had been completed and removed the pen drive before moving to the window. The container looked so different with one bale on the roof and the two rolled bales of straw protruding from the door space, like two black buttocks. It lifted her mood.

***

Shaw came to. His hand moved instinctively to the wound. The throbbing throughout his head seemed to run down his whole body. The swelling around his right eye felt huge. His left eye opened, the right remained closed but the darkness was complete. Holding a hand close to his open eye was pointless. For a moment he thought he had been blinded but he could not remember how, his head swam, a mix of pain and confusion.

Rolling onto his back he brought his hands to his face and cupped his eyes gently. *Where the hell am I? Kerry, is she alright? Has there been an accident?* The thoughts followed one after the other, confused broken images that seemed to make no sense as he tried making some semblance of his befuddled, painful state. What appeared most confusing was the word *daddy.* The word swam into his mind repeatedly before vanishing, each time it reappeared it seemed to be spoken more loudly and became more pronounced. Slowly, as if a thick mist was finally lifting, his memory began to return. He first remembered the clay head, the photographs and then

Kerry, the evil expression, the capriciousness of mood.

Moving his hands like a blind man feeling his way, he rolled to his left before managing to sit. The wall, cold and metallic was close. Shuffling he moved to lean against it. His breathing slowed as he tried to come to terms with his thoughts. He sensed the floor had changed – wood had replaced stone – he was in a different room. There was a stench, too, strong, like disinfectant or bleach but also the musky smell of straw. He closed his eye and breathed deeply.

"Is there anyone here?" His voice raised enough to increase the throbbing in his head. There was no response. Lifting a hand, he let it fall against the metal wall, a slap that echoed bringing with it even more distress.

"You're back in the land of the living." The male voice was calm, almost monotonous.

"Hello, yes, yes. Can you help me? I'm in the dark here. Is there a light?"

"I can bring you light."

Immediately the LED bulb was switched on. The intensity startled Shaw making him close his eye and turn away briefly until he felt his vision adjust. Staring ahead he saw the opposite wall, the graffiti daubed with the same words that had confronted Jones. He read them before turning to the screen that was positioned across the corner.

"I'll give you ten minutes of light that's all. Explore, Dr Shaw, familiarise yourself with your surroundings."

Shaw staggered to his feet. "Who are you? Where's Kerry? Why am I here?"

"Who, where, why? Because, Dr Shaw, you are a pervert, maybe not a paedophile in the true sense, but then you might be. That could well be one of your hidden secrets. Maybe you just take advantage of those who seek your help and trust. Look at the photographs on the screen and refresh the memory trapped within your now confused brain."

Standing, he looked around. One wall was made up of plastic covered straw, a convex wall that protruded into the space. He found his balance and moved to the screen as instructed. Looking behind, he saw the camping toilet, then he looked at the photographs. They were of both Gülen and Kerry. There was a contrast in the girls' expressions covering all aspects of his relationship with them – laughing, studying but the majority were of a sexual nature.

"Where did you get these?"

"There's always one victim in every abusive relationship and you found two with these girls. The girls kept them. Candid shots that are proof of your guilt."

"And you are?" A degree of anger was clear in his response.

"I spoke with Gülen some time ago, your Gülen, the one in the photographs. She told me everything. She told me how you knew about her father's abuse which she had suffered since she was a young girl. You were aware her father allowed her to travel if she remained complicit, kept the sordid affair secret. You knew he moved to Germany to raise the money for her education in exchange for her silence. You were privy and still you groomed her, abused her insecurity as a student. She felt like an imposter, a syndrome that many students experience, a weakness you can use for your own gratification. She trusted you with her dreadful secrets and yet ..."

"I helped her focus on her studies, I took her to another level. Tried to make her move on."

"And in return?"

He shook his head although he knew no one else was present.

"She wasn't the first either. She knew that, another student who left had received your guiding hand before her. She took that first photograph. She gave me others. Mobile phones are so useful. You even helped her find a flat, a love nest. She told me that too. Who paid for that, Dr Shaw?"

Nothing was said. Shaw looked at the offending photographs.

"The real trouble came when she walked in and found you with Kerry. Remember? Kerry was face down across your desk and you, where were you? Helping her focus on her studies but then she wasn't a student, was she? She was someone who needed a bit of help. You saw the photograph, you ripped it into pieces and that was just like she felt, torn apart, broken for yet another time in her short life. She was in bits just like those fragments that lay scattered on the floor. Did you pay Gülen to keep quiet, is that why you met with her on a number of occasions after you'd run away to seek impunity in another university?"

There was a long pause before Shaw nodded. "We had an agreement. Kerry had gone already and she agreed to leave too and say nothing if I paid what she asked. In return I would keep my reputation."

"So, the question you must ask yourself is, who made your ceramic head? Who made Jones's hands and head? Who would have the skill? You do know Gülen has disappeared, you know she's not coming back?"

"Are you Jones, Bernard Jones?" Shaw asked, an immediate fear creeping into his voice. "Kerry was a grown woman, not a child and she wasn't your daughter. She also shared with me what you put her through. She forgave you. She's given you a second chance so why are you now tormenting me?"

"Bernard Jones will never come back either. How can any girl be safe with a man like him within the community? He was still spreading his evil web even after Kerry left, even with Gülen. No, he'll not be back, not amongst the living at least. You asked who I am. I'm Derek Coulson, ceramist, artist and someone who cares deeply about Gülen. Shocked, Dr Shaw?"

The light was switched off, the thick dark returned and with arms outstretched Shaw fumbled his way towards where he believed the wall to be. He lowered himself, sat and tried to put what he had just heard into some sort of perspective.

Chapter 23

"Shaw drives a Lexus 4x4, metallic silver," April announced as she added the registration number to the boards before moving to a map of the area marking the ANPR sightings and placing a coloured magnetic circle at locations – the A59, Harrogate town centre, two places on the outskirts of Ripon. She added the dates and times. The date for each sighting was the same and the times showed the car's route. There was an indication that the driver had stopped for some time between Harrogate and Ripon. It had been two days since the last log entry. Traffic patrols had been alerted as well as parking wardens and PCSOs. She checked the ANPR locations within North Yorkshire identifying the areas which were not covered.

Brian Smirthwaite came over and joined April at the desk. He tracked the route pausing at the last known location with his pen and noted the possible roads Shaw might have travelled from that point without being picked up again. There were advantages to living in the Yorkshire Dales and he could name many, but professionally, the amount of countryside and small roads made disappearing from the system too easy.

"Anywhere from there across to there when travelling in this direction and double the area from east to west. Farms, remote buildings that are only used every blue moon, villages, quarries, woodland, you name it, they're all possibilities. The good news is, April, he hasn't left using any major routes, so, he's still in the area."

"Providing he's driving the car." April's face said it all. "He's not in trouble with the police so realistically he should turn up somewhere. He's not, I assume, in hiding. It's the length of time taken to get from here to the centre of Ripon, just over four hours. Where did he stop?"

"Ripley, strangely he could have come off the A61 and gone to Fountains." He looked up at April. "Could there be a connection? To be honest there are so many possibilities where the roads are devoid of ANPR. We could check for CCTV in Ripley and work from there. It's like tightening a noose, a bloody big one!"

"Get Dan Grimshaw to check it out. There's the pub, The Ram's Head"

"Boar's Head."

"Right, The Boar's Head. There's bound to be some security looking onto the outside."

***

Park's enquiries at the university were brief. Dr Shaw had taken time away for a family matter. He should, according to the notes held, be returning in three days' time. It was all matter of fact and yet the administrator still appeared to be concerned.

"It's such a shame. Serious family illness is not

something any of us finds comfortable, I believe it's his mother. He's such a caring man with our students. We're lucky to have him on the team. I do hope your being here is not bad news."

Park gave little away. He thanked her, smiled, left his card asking for her to call him should Shaw return early and moved away to join the uniformed officer from the local police who had accompanied him. "Bloody convenient. Strangely, his parents live in Spain and as far as we know he's not left the country. The first thing we checked."

Within twenty minutes the pair parked outside his home. It had been discovered the house was rented and the landlord was waiting on their arrival. Park showed the warrant and after a brief discussion Park and the landlord entered. The officer was asked to call on either side and check with the neighbours. There was no security alarm. They checked each room on the ground floor. It was orderly but not tidy. Books were piled on many surfaces in one room. Upstairs was the same. Park stood in the bedroom. The room was immaculate. He stared at the painting above the bed.

"Is the house let furnished?" he asked the landlord. Park studied the canvas.

"Yes, but personal items like that painting belong to Dr Shaw. There's some in his study. He teaches art. Many are stacked against the wall. He keeps his painting stuff in the conservatory."

The painting reminded Park of the American artist, Jackson Pollock. The frameless canvas was painted dark blue and made up of what appeared to be splashes and splodges in a variety of different colours, some smudging and others blending, to him it looked like the after effects of a disaster. "Not my cup of tea!" It was signed *Shaw* and dated *2015*. One particular area drew Park's attention. In an area splashed black there appeared to be a small hole.

"Take that side and lift it from the wall, please," Park requested.

The landlord frowned but he did as he was instructed laying it on the bed face down. A small, black rectangular box was attached to the canvas by black tape. He knew just what it was. Leaving the painting he checked the wardrobes that ran down one side of the room. In the first was a large safe.

"Yours?"

"No."

There were more paintings but also clothes. Park moved each hanger sideways before moving to the next wardrobe door. He did the same but stopped at one holding a suit cover. Removing it he lay it on the bed, swiftly unzipping it. It held women's clothes, five different items. He checked the labels, they varied in size.

"I think Dr Shaw was a ladies' man," the landlord said folding his arms as if to separate himself from the intrusion. "Is that a camera?" He pointed to the box on the back of the painting.

Park shrugged his shoulders but was non-committal.

"However, I never had him pegged as a pervert. Is that why you're here?"

"No, we need to speak with him about another matter. What goes on in his house is not our concern. However, it might be yours. For the moment I'll expect your full discretion. None of what you've seen here goes out of these four walls. Is that understood?" Park stared at the man leaning against the far wall.

"Indeed. Not one word. I value my privacy and my businesses." Park's insinuated threat had been received and understood.

The painting was returned after a number of photographs of the room and its contents had been taken. The house was locked.

"My contact details. If he should return, I'd value a swift call no matter what time. Please remember, nothing about what you have witnessed." Park nodded, thanked him and walked to the car where his colleague was waiting.

"Anything?"

"Nothing from number seventeen but the lady there has much to say. Shaw seems to have a few of his students call on him at home and not during the normal hours you'd expect, female too. She has a camera that points to her gate. It's to protect her car, really. It also covers his gate. Motion activated. She showed me the images of his leaving very, very early. He was carrying a holdall as if he was going away for a few days. He normally only takes a computer case when he goes to the university. She kindly printed a still from the video."

Park looked at it. "Did he tell her where he was going?"

"They no longer speak. He thinks she spies too much. Her words!"

"The pot calling the kettle if you ask me."

***

Derek Coulson sat at the kitchen table eating a bowl of

Weetabix as Kerry sat next to him. She fumbled with the USB stick turning it over in her fingers. He occasionally fed her a spoonful of his cereal. “You’re like a cuckoo, Kerry Jones.”

“That’s why you’re the only man I’ve loved, you give without expecting anything in return.” Kerry slid her hand on his. “Not long. I never thought I’d have the courage to trust someone like I trust you.”

Derek smiled, put his cereal bowl into the sink and ran a little water. The kettle on the camping stove began to whistle.

“Tea? We have no coffee.” He took two mugs from the kitchenette. “We have no sugar either.” He raised his eyebrows and immediately saw guilt cross her face. “I’d call it perfect planning.” Her smile returned.

The dark brown liquid steamed as Kerry wrapped her hands around the mug. “Let’s hope we’ve planned all of this well too.” The uncertainty in her eyes was clearly evident and Derek noticed a slight shake to her hands.

“We’ll be fine. I’ll have this and then get on the forklift. The last part is always the hardest. I’m not expecting any of the farm folk in the yard now. I’ll need a hand when you’ve added his confession onto the USB drive. Then everything, and I mean everything, needs to be brought to the barn.” He drank what remained in his mug and added it to the sink. “We’ll be fine.” He moved across, kissed the top of her head and went into the yard.

Within minutes she heard the forklift start but remained still gripping the mug. For a moment she was the girl standing naked in her bedroom, her father kneeling before her whilst running his hands over her small developing breasts. She could hear his every word even now, like a delayed yet sinister echo from the past – *Cinders is slowly becoming my very own Cinderella. How beautiful you are.* His hands had roamed further and she could feel the nausea bubble in her throat, a feeling she had experienced many times. The tears ran down her cheeks as if purging the childhood guilt, a guilt that was promulgated on her not being good enough, not loving as much as he had demanded.

Kicking back the chair she stood and threw the mug without thought of where it would land. It hit the kitchenette striking one of the two dimpled glass windows positioned in the upper doors. The shattering of glass brought her back to the present. She hung her head and controlled her anger and frustration. As she calmed, she remembered the first time she had met Derek. Gülen had extended a hand of friendship after seeing her in Shaw's office. She had waited for her and spoken first. There was no anger, no inquisition. It was as if she knew what she had lived through and like kindred spirits there was a commonality, an understanding that is only found in the abused. Even though it was invisible to many it was crystal clear to those who had lived in the same darkness and with the same guilt. Derek understood too, he had this place, his bolt hole when he left university, remote and yet beautiful. He had an agreement with a farm worker named John, he had explained.

Kerry moved to the window and stared through the net curtains into the yard. They had been right, it was a haven, an oasis of calm and security and she had been wise to listen. Few people came, and those that did were in and out, workers on a mission unless it was John. She had decided, like Gülen, to remain anonymous, a ghost in the house, unseen and unheard and it was in this building their secrets were shared, their demons laid to rest.

The forklift moved across the yard and dropped another huge round bale behind those already blocking the doors of the container, the torn areas of black plastic wrapping flapped like rooks' wings. The busy, yellow ant, scooped more straw bales and began linking a trail from one to the other until they reached the wall of the cottage. The last few seemed to surround the Lexus and one was positioned next to an old diesel tank that had long since been emptied. Derek's old van, her van, the stubborn bitch of a van was left alone. The other car he had used on occasion sat within the barn.

Kerry went into the yard before squeezing through a gap in the newly constructed straw wall and entered the small building to the left of the container. There was an old folding camping chair, an iPad wired to a wall socket and linked to a lead that ran on a short catenary wire, bridging the gap between the shed in which she stood and the container. She switched on the tablet as she let her finger rest momentarily on the light switch set onto the shelf. The simple connection between camera and tablet required only a cable and a power source. As she flicked the switch the inside of the container was visible on the screen.

Shaw was curled on the floor. The damage she had inflicted to his eye was clearly visible but she felt no regret. She saw him move. Using both hands he pushed himself into a seated position.

"Hello, Callum, it's Kerry. I just wanted to say goodbye. We're leaving soon."

She heard him speak but his words were indistinguishable. He spoke again. This time his words becoming clearer. “And me? The fool who trusted you. Am I going to leave too?”

“When I was little my father told me that when you die you either go up to heaven or down to hell depending on whether you had been good or bad, hell seemed to feature a lot with me unless, of course, I loved Daddy a lot. It seemed so easy as a child as there was no sideways moves only up or down. Above me there was the sky in all its glory, the colours, the clouds and at night the stars. That way seemed so exciting. Down below was the dirt, the worms, the rocks and stones. He told me to look beyond that as above the stars was a place of beauty, where God lives and where the good girls go and find everlasting happiness and kindness. Below, below, Callum, is a place filled with fire and brimstone and occupied with the unredeemed and the damned.”

“Kerry. I am sorry. Truly. Now stop messing about. I'm hurt and need to get back. I'll not mention any of this if you'll just get Coulson to let me go.”

“We've created hell here on earth and just like we took Daddy's breath away we are ...” she paused. “The one good thing in all of this is that he and soon you will never groom or abuse again.”

Her finger flicked off the light switch and the screen went black. She could hear her name being called over and over again. Even when she unplugged the iPad and left the building, the echoing pleas seemed to ring around the yard and grow louder until they stopped altogether. Derek saw her leave and waved before offering a thumbs up sign. She reciprocated.

Chapter 24

Stuart Park entered the Incident Room as soon as he returned from Lancashire.

"Look at these."

He spread out the photographs taken of the various rooms but seemed eager to concentrate on those featuring the bedroom. "It's a shot of a camera that was taped behind that painting and I'd bet it was positioned to film the bed and all that went on in it. He has a large safe in the wardrobe. After discovering the camera, I really think we need to look in there. I wonder what your average university professor needs to keep locked securely away? And then we have these." He placed the photographs of the clothing. "Women's but not his size. That would've been too easy. They're various sizes and I guess owned by different young women, students maybe."

April chipped in. "You reported that the university believes he's been called away owing to a family illness, his mother, and yet she lives a life of sun and sangria in Benidorm according to our investigation. We also know he hasn't left the country to date. What's more interesting is according to CCTV he was in Ripley two days ago. Dan

Grimshaw tracked down the video and is making further enquiries. It should be with us shortly. Dr Shaw was with a young woman. Her identity is still to be determined."

"Seems a common denominator with him. She's definitely not his mother then?"

A few giggles erupted but were soon calmed as Cyril entered, his facial expression clearly demonstrating he was in no mood for hilarity.

"Well done, Stuart. The pieces of this credible jigsaw are slowly coming together and if we're good at what we do they should go back to form a totally clear picture. April suggested the police helicopter be called to overfly the area in which we believe Shaw to be but unless we have another body or a 999 link to any of the missing, we have little chance owing to costs. It's down to sound policing from the information that continues to emerge. Anything from the published requests after showing his photograph?"

Harry Nixon shook his head. "We've put out the number plate and description of the car. Local news, both radio and TV will run it."

"It seems a strange, maybe bizarre, coincidence that both he and Jones are or were located within three miles of each other. How far is Ripley from West Gate carpark?"

April quickly checked on Google maps. "6.9 miles. Thirteen minutes in a car."

"Jones's van travelled to the place undetected and it may well have been after dark but he was in a stolen van. The more forensic evidence we receive gives us the confidence to say with more certainty he died somewhere else and then taken there. Was Shaw going to that same unknown location, the place where Jones may have met his death? If so, he appears to be there willingly and if it's true he's with a young woman, he may well be being led by his dick?" Cyril tossed his glasses onto the table.

April looked up surprised at her boss's crude choice of words.

"Request dash cam footage of anyone travelling either way on that day on the route that was mapped by the ANPR. I need that information out with an urgent plea to the public tagged to it. Get more people on the ground in Ripley knocking on doors. Grimshaw can co-ordinate that as he's there. Organise a search. However, it's best to identify any isolated farm buildings or caravans. It's a wildcard, but if I'm right, Dr Callum Shaw is not going where he thinks he is."

***

Kerry slipped the iPad onto the driver's seat of the old van alongside a few other personal items before returning to the cottage. She collected any bits of clothing surplus to requirements, also the bedding and the photographs that were pinned on the battens in the back room. She made a number of treks to the barn before taking another look around each room.

The shattered fragments of her father's ceramic head still lay where they had fallen. One piece comprising a large part of the left side of the face stared up from the flagged floor. *He's looking from hell*, she thought as a smile touched her lips. The hammer was still where she had left it and with one swing the piece scattered over much of the floor.

She collected the two ceramic hands and popped them into the box that contained Jones's clay head. This box was placed with the other items. The head, however, would be placed in the Lexus. Derek was breaking up a bale he had dropped by the door to the cottage and was leading a trail of straw through the kitchen.

"When you've dumped that in the barn, Kerry, cover it with a good deal of straw, then help me here."

***

Smirthwaite entered the Incident Room holding some notes.

"Latest forensics from the suicide. The DNA makes fascinating reading. Clear traces were found from both missing women, Gülen Köse and Kerry Jones. Passenger seat and seat belt and some limited contact on the driver's seat. It's suggested that neither drove the vehicle. They've managed to eliminate the real owner's DNA."

Cyril moved to the whiteboards and wrote the word, *Retribution*, before saying the word slowly. "Retribution. Punishment inflicted on someone as a vengeance for an act they have committed in the past. Are we simply looking at entrapment and possible double murder? Did the two women know each other and if so, how?"

"Has Kerry been in Harrogate all this time?" Smirthwaite chipped in. "The best place to hide is where people least expect to find you."

"Did Shakti ever trace a link between students who went to that college training media makeup and Kerry Jones?" Cyril asked.

"We know she didn't attend but I don't think we went as far as interviewing the students to see if they knew her or knew anyone who did know Kerry."

"You see my thinking here, April?"

"Identity change?"

He nodded. "Clever makeup can change a face so easily, even a person's sex."

As Cyril finished his sentence, she nodded, moved away and picked up the phone. A call to the manager and a copy of the girl's photograph could be easily distributed amongst the students and hopefully should elicit a swift response.

Smirthwaite added more forensic evidence. "Remember there was no trace of the soil found in West End carpark on Jones's shoes? Well, the boffins have found a match of material within whatever soil was present between the heels and the soles and the mattress. Also, minute particles of straw were trapped within it and the same with the outer fabric of the mattress. They know it had been resting on its side, leaning against straw for some time and even though it was probably wrapped with plastic there was still residue trapped. There was, however, no animal faeces within the soil taken from both shoes and the van's pedals and carpet that would be found if he'd walked in a field or farmyard where animals were present but there was haylage."

"A needle, then, is what we are looking for, Brian? And if we find that we have our place?"

Chapter 25

"Put the bag and the USB pen drive where we agreed and make sure your prints are not on the stick and the bag. Get Tommy and keep him safe. There's a lidded basket in the van. Make sure any food for him is put in there too. I've emptied the kitchenette of our food. Did you not like the glass in that unit?" He turned and winked at her. "Me neither. When that's done, move the van out of the yard and down the track. I'll meet you there."

Derek looked round the cottage for one last time. The quantity of loose straw was spread liberally throughout each room and on the stairs. A rectangular bale was placed near the gas cylinder that fed the camping stove, which was half full. Moving out, he crossed the yard keeping to one side of the installed straw wall that bridged the buildings to the barn. His penultimate stop was to the boot of his car that was parked in the Dutch barn between the combine and the remaining round, stacked bales.

Opening the boot, he withdrew four large plastic containers one at a time. He took them placing them strategically at key points along the straw wall, the last one was left in the kitchen of the cottage. Returning to the open barn, he paused for a few minutes as if in conversation and then unhooked some overalls from the barn's vertical frame. As he moved away, he brought his fingers to his lips then dropped them. To an onlooker it would appear as if he were blowing a kiss into the air to a lover.

Once clad in the overalls he began pouring the fluid from the containers onto the straw wall. He worked methodically and carefully until finally he went to into the cottage spreading the fluid in a continuous line following the straw trail.

***

The Incident Room was even more busy. Messages now seemed to come from Grimshaw at regular intervals. He sent screen shots of the CCTV taken from the external cameras of the pub. It was clearly Callum Shaw.

In Ripley it was a chance call at one of the cottages bordering the road that energised Dan.

"We have so many visitors here, I guess you could say it's a haven for them being off the main road and what with the castle, that draws in so many. I flew my drone that day. I fly from the field at the back, I'm learning if I'm honest. I can show you what footage I have but I can't recall seeing a silver car. It's one of the most common colours, silver. Did you know that?"

Dan did not answer and was eager to see the footage. To his relief the search in the laptop files was not as arduous as he thought it might be.

"This is from the date you requested. It was early morning but it was a good day as the visibility was perfect."

He ran the clip.

"Can you pause there?" The captured video stopped. He pointed to the car that was parked at the side of the road. "Just zoom in on that if you can."

"That's nearly outside my front door."

Dan scrutinised the still image locating the few people in the area concentrating on the man standing by the statue of the boar. "Can you zoom in more?"

"Sorry, the camera is not as good as I'd hoped when I bought the drone but … shall I run it on?"

The recording started and they watched another vehicle pull up behind the silver car Dan believed to be Shaw's. Unfortunately, the drone was moving away above the church and within seconds the cars and the person by the statue were out of shot.

"Is that all you have?" Dan sounded disappointed.

"I have a little of when I brought it back to the home point."

The second file was found. "Here we are. The silver car's still there as is the van."

"Please pause it. Zoom in if you can."

"There, that's the same man walking with someone by the castle entrance." The drone owner was getting very excited. "There are four other people in the shot too."

"Please start it."

The drone just passed over the houses and descended.

"Any more?"

"Sorry, limited memory on the micro card. It's all about memory and I forget to press to stop recording sometimes. Flying and pressing buttons can be very confusing when you're a novice."

"No, just perfect. I need your permission to get these in to our digital forensics. The tech people may well be able to enhance the quality."

Within ten minutes the footage had been sent to control along with a request for digital forensics to see if enhancement would be possible. The video was also sent to Cyril.

Cyril watched it on his phone with a commentary from Dan to highlight what he was looking at. He paused it as he looked down at Ripley Church, the place where he was married but quickly moved on.

Chapter 26

Derek Coulson left the cottage and climbed onto the forklift, raised the fork and ran it deliberately into the straw wall until the horizontal forks were buried. Climbing from it he removed his overalls and tossed them onto the seat. From his jean pocket he removed a Zippo lighter, flipped the lid and a flick of his thumb brought a strong flame. It took less than two minutes to light the fluid-soaked straw in a number of places. The flames burned invisibly initially but soon the combusting straw was quick to smoke. His final location was the kitchen. Once the straw was burning with some force, he tossed the lighter onto the unit holding the camping stove.

Shaw was sitting in total darkness. He found the straw protruding within the space making for a more comfortable back rest. He had heard the vehicle moving outside but now there was silence. His eye still throbbed but his head had now cleared. It was only then the realisation that he was alone, that they had left, flashed through his mind. As if by instinct, he rolled to face the plastic covered bale of straw and like the blind man he had become through the lack of light, let his hands feel and discover the wall's dimensions.

He spoke out loud to himself as he thought of the children's story of *The Three Little Pigs*

"I can't go through steel but I can pull away the straw."

He started slowly tearing pieces of the plastic and then attacking the straw. It was not as easy as he had hoped but it was moving. Concentrating on the area where the bale hit the edge of the steel, a line that marked the place where the doors had once been seemed the most logical place. If he could remove a little, he might be able to squeeze through.

"I'll tear and pull and this house will open." For the first time since being struck by the hammer he felt a degree of hope. His spirits lifted.

Coulson moved away towards the track that led out of the yard. The van would be a hundred yards away. He wanted to see the fire, to watch the straw bridge he had constructed carry the flames and link the buildings and consume the cottage. More importantly he wanted to see the shipping container sit within a ring of flame. The growing inferno brought with it an increase in the flow of air that was dragged towards the fire. Small branches of the nearby bushes began to sway.

Shaw paused. He could hear something he had not noticed before. It was a crackling. He continued to pull away more of the straw at the edge that sat about a metre into the space. He could feel the distance between the steel and the edge; it was decreasing, he was winning. Pulling with greater enthusiasm he knew he was approaching the edge. As another clump came away, he saw it and his heart leapt. A thin, yellow strip of light flushed into the darkness.

"Yes! Yes! Yes!"

He began pulling at the bale with a renewed eagerness. It was as he dragged more away he saw the first tendrils of white smoke, wisps that blunted the light and brought with it the stench of burning hay to his nostrils. He rested a hand against the steel wall and felt the warmth. The crackling was now louder and the warmth he felt was not only that from his exertion but from what was happening outside. Kerry's words came immediately to mind – *below, Callum, is a place filled with fire and brimstone and occupied with the unredeemed and the damned.* He then recalled the final words she had spoken not an hour ago – *We've created hell here on earth and just like we took Daddy's breath away we are ...*

"Going to take yours." His words were but a whisper but they stirred an inner fear and yet a determination to see her wrong. "I'll be damned if you do."

With added panic he tore and ripped at the straw, the light grew and with it the smoke.

Coulson stood and watched the wall begin to crumble in places as the flames leapt higher; the milky-yellow straw turning to black. The bales in the barn were also alight as was the cottage. Flames were clearly visible within the upstairs windows. Plumes of smoke rose quickly, grey intermingled with black as the developing heat caused it to spiral upwards with a greater urgency. The stench grew along with the increasing draught.

He turned and walked down the lane. The smoke would now be attracting the wrong attention and they needed to leave. As he climbed into the driver's seat of the van, he glanced at the plastic bag hanging from the crooked gatepost. Kerry had her feet on the dashboard and was staring ahead. He slipped his hand onto her leg.

"It'll soon be over and done with. We need to be a long way from here. Ready?"

She turned and smiled. "Ready. Thank you for enabling me to trust again."

Sweat began to bead over most of Shaw's face. He removed his jumper, suddenly remembering that he had not bothered with his shirt when he had dressed. His feet were bare too. "When was that?" He had lost all track of time. As he pulled away more of the straw, he saw the first pieces of incinerated ash enter, drift and fall, captured in the growing light. The far bale was glowing around the edge, the lower lip too was changing and deep red as the fire seemed to create a halo around the bales.

"Oh shit! No! I'm sorry. Make it stop, please, Kerry. Kerry, make it stop!"

Moving away on his backside he slithered to the far end of the container. The glow from the burning bales illuminated the small space lighting the words written on the wall. He eyes rested on the main word – *Pandora.*

Thick smoke began to fog his vision and his eye started to sting. He rubbed it but there was no relief. The heat was now intense, the smoke made breathing difficult. He coughed and began to retch. He could not keep his eye open. Curling into a ball gave him a moment's relief.

… and just like we took Daddy's breath away … Kerry's words came back, drifting like the smoke within his failing consciousness. "Please!" The word reverberated around the metal box. The plywood floor began to smoulder, acrid fumes added to the choking atmosphere. His hair began to singe, but he felt nothing as he gasped for air, sucking in

the poisonous fumes in even deeper gulps. Within seconds, Shaw exhaled his final breath.

The van left the lane and moved towards the A1M. A petrol station would be their first stop, but not for some time. They would not stop again for many hours.

Chapter 27

The huge plume of smoke appeared dark grey against the blue late afternoon sky and seemed to stretch at an angle towards the east. Small pieces of straw ash drifted and swirled like grey snowflakes before settling over a broad expanse. Some, if lit, were extinguished on hitting the ground and others burned brightly before dying. A number of people had seen the smoke but no one had taken the initiative until one of the workers from the neighbouring farm drove over to investigate. He stopped on the wider of the two tracks before entering the yard, the same route taken by the heavy farm machinery and particularly the combine.

Had he come a moment later he would not have seen the gas canister linked to the camping stove within the cottage explode and launch itself through the kitchen window before landing halfway into the yard, its jagged, open steel skin smoking.

The barn was well alight, the car and combine wrapped in the intense flames, flames that brought a heat shimmer to the whole area visually distorting the steel uprights to the barn as well as the distant woods and fields that ran away behind. It was then he saw the second car, the windows had shattered and the tyres melted leaving a mass of wire where the rubber had once been; now it was a mass of protruding steel that wrapped the wheels in like a red hot cage.

"Fucking hell!" His two words summed up the scene perfectly, yet he was totally unaware of the trapped secrets hidden within the inferno.

Taking out his phone he dialled 999 requesting fire and police.

***

"Large fire, isolated farm near to the Old Melmerby Ordnance Depot." Owen leaned into the room. "It's well off the nearest road. According to the report coming in there's a good deal of haylage on fire within a barn along with some small buildings. The cottage is semi-derelict and according to the caller, unoccupied. The owner has assured us there's no fuel or fertilizer stored at the site. Emergency services are in attendance initially from Ripon but Boroughbridge and Masham crews are on standby. Large hay fires can be difficult to control and fully extinguish depending on a number of factors, as they can stay lit for days. We should get a report as soon as our people arrive. I've made them very much aware of what we're looking for."

"I assume the owner or the site manager will be in attendance?" Cyril stared at the computer screen and enlarged the area around the ordnance depot. "I take it that's now obsolete?"

"Well and truly. 1969. It's used as an industrial site now. More storage within the old munitions' sheds than anything else."

"Did we check this area after finding Jones?"

Owen shook his head. "It's not considered isolated as people use the place."

Cyril looked at Owen, a degree of incredulity clearly stamped across his face.

***

Kerry had slept for the first two hours and woke as they approached Alnwick, Northumberland. Derek had decided to drive the A19 rather than the busier A1M. It was his gut instinct on arriving at the motorway junction. He felt the road less travelled might be the wiser route, time was not important, anonymity was.

"Where are we?" Kerry stretched and sat up looking sideways before turning to check on Tommy who had remained curled within the basket.

"The A1 near Alnwick."

"The castle!" She turned and looked at him, her face suddenly that of a child. "It was used in the first two Harry Potter films. It's a magical place."

"There's another castle I'll show you. It's rugged and beautiful and I hope we can stay nearby for a few nights."

"Derek, when Gülen left just before Shaw arrived, where did she go?"

"I dropped her with relatives in Leeds who were taking her to London where she has cousins. They have a few businesses, barbers' shops and a restaurant. She said she'd stay there and then see where life took her."

"Were you not bitter about the break-up? Angered by

her as much as you were with Shaw for his advances and influence and maybe her weaknesses?"

There was a long pause and she watched him chew his lip as if to stop it quivering.

"Sorry, didn't mean to open old wounds."

"I realised she'd been hurt well before I met her and Shaw seemed to offer her stability not only emotionally but also professionally. I could see it coming but I didn't predict he'd up sticks and go. What hurt most was he kept seeing her, giving her false hope. He abused her like he abused you. It was only when she walked in on you and him, did she realise his depravity."

"She was kind to me. She helped me see the light and brought me to your place." She slipped her hand onto his thigh. "I never really said thank you or to her."

"She was kind to you. I was angry with her but also angry with what he'd done. It was then I got her away to a friend's caravan near Harrogate where she happened to meet your bloody father." His words stopped abruptly as if suddenly realising something that he had failed to see before. "You two didn't contrive that meet ..." He turned and looked at her.

Kerry squirmed a little as she turned to look out of the window. She had not been prepared for the direct question and she hoped her reaction was not obvious. "Like me, she seemed to attract the wrong kind of man. When I left home, I was desperate for support. That desperation brings with it many dangers. We talked about it afterwards. She didn't know, of course, and she was fine when it was a platonic friendship and then when he tried it on at bloody work it all became real! We were at the farm then. I knew it was him. I saw his photograph on her phone. I warned her. She was already aware of what he'd done to me and she had told me her story, her suffering as a child. We cried together." Her words flowed as if carrying both truth and lies.

"Justice has been served. Now we just have to disappear and create a new life." Derek spoke slowly as if he fully understood the task that was before them.

***

Cyril stood some distance away from the farmyard. Firefighters pulled apart and spread the blackened bales as more water dowsed the glowing interiors. The more they pulled in more oxygen that immediately fed the glowing embers causing them to flare again. The Senior Fire Officer pointed out what was being done.

"As far as we know from the drone footage there are four vehicles on site, two cars, one forklift, you can see it there, and a combine. There's also a small shipping container behind the car and yes, that is what remains of a Lexus. Significantly, we believe we have a fatality within the container. From what we can ascertain, the entrance was blocked by bales of straw and that area was the only entry and exit point. There was also a bale placed on the roof. It was clearly a deliberate act. There's also the remains of a generator to the rear of the container. From a first brief survey there's nobody in the cottage but once we have everything under control and it's safe to do so we'll be investigating further. It will be forty-eight hours before we can safely say it's secure and then Forensics can come in. What I can tell you, Cyril, is that all of this is arson. You can see how the bales have been linked to ensure the whole place is connected particularly the container."

The thought of being trapped within a steel box and roasted alive made him shiver.

As the smouldering bales were being pulled out of the Dutch barn away from the yard one burst into flames.

The officer tapped Cyril on the shoulder. "You can see from that the reason we need to be cautious."

Cyril moved further away and leaned on his car. The body in the container was likely to be that of Shaw and he believed, like Bernard Jones, he had been enticed there. A firefighter approached. "We've found this hanging on the gatepost on the far drive." He handed it to Cyril before turning and walking back to the fire.

The polythene bag contained a USB pen drive. Cyril held it between finger and thumb.

Chapter 28

Three days later

The packed briefing watched in silence as Owen went through the contents of the USB drive that had been downloaded. The photographs showed both Gülen Köse and Kerry Jones. They listened to the one-sided confessions of both men. Cyril reflected on the accusations brought to their attention by ShadowLink and wondered if his hatred of paedophile gangs should be reviewed. They seemed to have a stronger finger on the pulse than the force.

"We've managed to open Shaw's safe. A laptop found contained a considerable number of images and videos."

He played some. Many depicted the same group of young women. There were forty-seven video recordings taken using the hidden cameras.

"There was another camera hidden in the shower area as well as a second located in the bedroom. It's clear those involved had no idea they were being abused in this way. We've managed to identify many of the individuals through the university. The sharp eyed amongst you will note that some videos and photographs were taken in a different location but the painting above the bed is the same, suggesting these were when he lived in the Leeds area. It's the same room as seen in the photographs on the drive here. Those videos also show the two missing women, Köse and Jones. What we don't know is how Köse ended up in Harrogate illegally and how she links with Bernard Jones. There's a suggestion it was pre-planned. This may well be supported by the discovery of minute DNA traces from both women found on the pen drive. The outer surfaces had been wiped but our techniques need very little to get a match. I'm of the opinion that both men were drawn to a honeytrap, a term I don't like but the evidence suggests they were at different times drawn to the one location where they met their deaths."

Cyril stood and moved to the front by the flat screen. He nodded to the officer by the computer.

"Thanks, Owen. CSI are presently searching the farm but we have these images. The body in the container we know to be that of Callum Shaw. Remnants of a chemical toilet were found inside near the body which suggests it was a holding cell. There was also some link to a stone shed next to the container, it's been suggested it housed electricity and maybe communications but most has been severely damaged."

He nodded and the image changed. Describing the image, he continued. "It's an internal shot of one of the container walls. I'm assured there is writing there." Another slide was shown and the marked colour change in the wall showed what appeared to be a shadow of some lettering.

"I'm told it reads *Pandora*."

Pausing, he let the ripple of conversation run around the gathering. "The container holding the sins of the world."

The next images appeared on the screen and ran one after the other. "Two ceramic heads, one smashed and two ceramic hands. All survived the fire in various states. These, we now firmly believe, were used to mould the silicon items we discovered. Shaw's ceramic head was located on the driver's seat of his car. The final piece of forensics suggests the container was used to kill Bernard Jones." Cyril nodded and a picture of a badly burned generator appeared.

"This was located a short distance from the container and residue of a similar pipe to that found at the site where he was found was also traced. It linked the generator to a small vent in the back of the container. He was poisoned using the exhaust gas."

An officer entered the room and walked towards Cyril, handing him a slip of paper. "Photographs are coming through, sir."

A second body has been found within the far corner of the barn and covered with one of the large straw bales. Partially burned but the upper torso is well preserved.

The vehicle …

Cyril read the first part of the note and then announced the discovery. Within minutes the forensic images came on screen. April looked at Owen and then at Cyril.

***

The shepherd's hut had immediately appealed to Kerry, it sat with four identical corrugated dwellings on wheels, each trapped within a small area of garden. It was, by contrast to the cottage, luxurious. Derek had rented it for four days. He would have liked longer but money constraints prevented that. The hot shower was something she had missed. The strip wash with cold water had been a necessary evil and the sacrifice had been worthwhile but that first shower seemed to slough the guilt, worry and anxiety she had carried since killing her father. It seemed to make it right.

Derek walked in with food from a local takeaway.

"I'd love to hear from Ghoul. I know she can't call and that makes it even more difficult. She should be in London now with her cousins. I hope she's as comfortable as we are."

Derek just smiled and offered her a slice of pizza.

"We have some more time here and then?" She tore a second slice.

"North. I need to find some temporary work."

***

"It's Gülen Köse's body. There is damage to the back of the skull and it was deliberately concealed beneath the bale. Owing to its location it was only partially burned. Autopsy results to follow. So far, there's no further evidence of more fatalities. We also know that the car discovered in the barn belonged to Derek Coulson, you will recall he was Köse's boyfriend and demonstrated concern over her relationship with Shaw. He's no longer at his address and according to neighbours has not been for some time."

Owen looked at Shakti who appeared lost and distracted.

"Having spoken to the owner he believed from his workers that the farm was empty and used as a storage area for the combine and haylage. However, an employee, a John Elmer, has been absent since the fire. Officers will be questioning him when he's been located."

"Why Gülen?" Shakti asked, more a reciprocal question that seemed to fall by the wayside. Her voice conveyed an inner anguish.

"Open mind everyone. Let's see what the autopsy has to offer. Owen, will you attend, please?"

Owen breathed a sigh.

"I want Coulson tracking, phone, bank. What are they driving now? Check for stolen vehicles at the time the van was taken. Put out an announcement to B&Bs, hotels, caravan sites. Flood his photograph nationally and I want it on as many platforms as possible. I'll do a talk to camera as soon as we finish here. Brian, please get our newsdesk to organise ASAP. I want her photograph on there too."

Chapter 29

Kerry lay on the bed. Tommy was curled at her feet. It was their final day and yet she was not ready to leave. The television was on but she was too interested in Tommy. The announcement including the name *Derek Coulson* made her look at the screen. There was a picture of Derek followed by images of the farm. Three more faces appeared on the screen. She grabbed the remote and turned up the volume.

"Two bodies have been recovered at the farm, those of Gülen Köse and Dr Callum Shaw. Their next of kin have been notified. The police are now looking to question Kerry Jones, aged twenty-one and Derek Coulson, twenty-five." Their photographs appeared side by side. "It is believed they may be travelling together." The various contact options filled the screen as she switched off the television.

Gülen, dead? The question ran haphazardly round her head. *She's in London.* She felt numb. The only explanation was it had to be Derek. Looking through the window she could not see him. She grabbed her small backpack, before opening the top drawer and removing all the money from his wallet.

"Sorry, Tommy. What has he done? I trusted him and it looks as though he's just like the rest."

Grabbing the van keys, she stumbled down the steps, through the gate and to the van. The first two turns failed to kick the motor into life.

"Come on, bitch!"

The vehicle started with its usual cough and emitted the puff of grey black smoke as if in protest. Within a minute she was heading out of the village.

***

"Credit card was last used as a deposit on a shepherd's hut in Northumberland. Crook's Hold Crofts in a village called Elford, just outside Bamburgh. They should leave tomorrow. The local force is on the way and taking all precautions. They communicated with the owner of the properties and, as of this morning, both occupants match the photographs of Jones and Coulson. However, Jones now wears glasses and her hair colour is different. They're in an old Citroen Van." Owen gave the registration. "It belongs to the employee who did a runner after the fire, John Elmer. He's been located and he's in for questioning. He got as far as his brother's in Holmfirth, admitted renting the cottage unbeknown to his boss and also his old van as a side line. Beer money were his very words."

"That might well turn into porridge!"

***

After returning to find the van gone, Coulson looked around

the hut. He searched for a note from Kerry but there was nothing. Tommy curled around his legs mewing constantly. Sliding the drawer, he noticed the money was gone. A sudden flash of blue light struck the mirror opposite the window, a strong and intense colour that immediately set his pulse racing. He knew what it was. He turned and opened the door and stood on the upper step. Three police vehicles were in the carpark and officers were placed strategically around the hut. He noticed one holding a German shepherd tightly to her leg and two others who might have firearms.

One approached. "Mr Derek Coulson?"

Coulson nodded.

The officer immediately cautioned him. "We need you to come with us. Is Kerry Jones in the hut?"

Coulson shook his head.

On the A1 just before Belford an unmarked police car followed the Citroen van, the number identified on the ANPR just outside Bamburgh. Within a mile, Kerry Jones would also be cautioned and arrested.

***

Owen sat with Dr Julie Pritchett following Gülen Köse's autopsy.

"She suffered serious cranium damage through a blunt trauma injury to the back of the skull but that wasn't the cause of death. She was then deliberately covered by three large bales of straw causing asphyxiation. She would have known nothing after the initial strike."

"How long ago?" Owen leaned forward.

"As I said in there, owing to the position of the body to the intense heat, which does affect the determination of such details, she's been dead about five days. As you saw, Owen, there is severe fire damage to the lower torso and crush and compression injuries to most of the body. She was also positioned face down prior to the placement of the bales which suggests she was struck where she fell. DNA has been confirmed for both Shaw and her. Looking at the trajectory of the blow it came from high right and the person would have been taller than her. That rules out Kerry Jones but rules in Derek Coulson. Samples taken from her clothing trapped in the breast area that was protected from the fire have been identified by Forensics to be a strand of a sweater owned and worn by Coulson when he was arrested. There's also a number of cat hairs."

"What would we do without the boffins? The minute elements of straw found in the soil sampled from Bernard Jones's shoes matches identically to that found in the yard even though much of the area was devastated by the fire. Something to do with the composition of clay that was peculiar to that specific farm."

"No matter how long I'm in this job I never seem to be able to comprehend the true extent of the determination of some to seek revenge no matter what the consequences. What did Confucius say, Owen?"

Owen shook his head.

'When you are beginning a journey of revenge, start by digging two graves.' On this occasion, he may well have been right. From what Cyril has said both the abuser and the abused died in the same place."

"Two women, both young and both abused as kids.

Hannah explained to me when I was telling her about them a while back. It's from Harry Potter. 'Harry was left to ponder in silence the depth to which girls would sink to get revenge.'

"If only they could have spoken about their abuse and received professional medical help who knows how their lives might have been improved. As it was, they kept their secrets trapped within."

***

April looked at Shakti as she nursed a mug of tea whilst staring at the photographs on the whiteboard.

"Are you alright, Shak?" April pulled up a chair and touched her hand.

Shakti burst into tears.

April let her cry.

"I've been there, April, I too was one of those girls from when I was young only it was my brother. I know why they push it away, bury it deeply as they're trapped in the confusion of what love really is. If someone you trust tells you something is normal and healthy when you don't have the life skills to question it, it becomes acceptable and yet uncomfortable." She paused looking directly at April. "I've carried it." She tapped her head and her chest. "Trapped here within me and this case has just lifted the lid."

"We can help you if you'll allow me, Shak. It's nothing for you to be ashamed of. Now it's out let's find you some real help to get rid of the guilt and trauma."

Shakti put the mug on the table and leaned to hug April. They were both in tears.

Chapter 30

The welcome Cyril and Julie received at Goldsborough Hall was generous and warm. There was something about the entrance, the glass chandelier, the height of the ceilings and warmth of the décor. Julie was shown to their room but Cyril made his way to the library stopping briefly to inspect the brass faced grandfather clock that ticked lugubriously in the semi-dark of the hallway. He checked his own watch, shook his wrist and checked again. The clock was still slow or his watch was fast.

The library was just as he remembered. The panelling, the heavy swag of the red velvet curtains and the beautiful stone fireplace. It was to one spot he wished to go and that was the window, the corner where the small pane was situated and where he had seen the encapsulated bubble. He let his finger caress the cold glass, feeling the swell of the extended surface created when the shape was formed those many years previously. "A fossilised whisper that may hold an ancient secret or maybe a wish … both made long ago." He spoke to no one but his thoughts were clearly on the two abused girls and their ruined lives. He turned and remembered the actor dead on the rug. If only all things in life were but a silly game, an ending where they would stand, resurrected to receive a warm round of applause before carrying on with their lives.

***

The dining room was quiet as they were shown to their table. Cyril sampled the wine and let the flavour roll round his mouth. He nodded and watched the waiter pour before leaving them.

"They admitted to the murders of both Bernard Jones and Callum Shaw. However, the main part was played by Coulson. He was the executioner. He also made the ceramic heads, the silicone copies, all unbeknown to the department, using materials belonging to the university. They had all hatched the plan. It seems as though Gülen's travelling to Harrogate was planned, part of the scheme to compromise her own father. It worked and was maybe a deal where she snared Jones and Kerry snared Shaw."

"So why kill the Turkish girl?"

"A silly argument. She didn't want Shaw dead when push came to shove. It was too late. It was impossible to let him go as by that time he knew about Kerry's father. What did Confucius say?"

"'Start digging two graves'." Julie was quick to answer. "I had that very conversation with Owen although Hannah pointed out to him how much people will sink to get revenge. I think it shook him. Speaking of Owen and knowing you have never been comfortable with the watch you bought after giving him yours, I have a present. It's not new. It's taken me a while to get it." She slid a small heart shaped box across the table and as he went to get it, she rested her hand on his. "You're a kind and honest man Cyril. This is with all my love and affection. I hope it gives you hours of pleasure."

He felt a lump in his throat as he looked at her. Curiosity was clearly in his eyes but in hers was excitement.

"Open it. It never belonged to Pandora."

Cyril lifted the lid and removed the deep red tissue paper. He brought it from the box with a degree of reverence – it was a Rolex Daytona wrist watch. The three silver edged dials set on a black face stared back.

"It's not new I'm afraid. There's a huge waiting list. Turn it over."

Cyril did as she requested. Engraved on the back were four words, *Our Time Is Now.* He looked at Julie and then at the watch. "I've always wanted one."

"I know. Now seemed the perfect time."

The dining room door opened and Clare Oglesby, the owner of the hotel entered with a waiter who was carrying a Champagne cooler. She smiled at Julie and then Cyril.

"With our compliments. I presume you like your watch DCI Bennett. We all hope you'll enjoy your stay and that it'll be less like work on this occasion and more relaxation."

He stood and shook her hand.

"Have you two ladies been plotting and scheming?"

"Indeed we have, but not for revenge."

Featured Artist

It gives me a great deal of pleasure when readers not only make positive comments about the series, but also about this feature I include in each book. Art is a passion of mine, a passion I transferred to Cyril Bennett and I love including art and artists within these tales. Wherever possible, I highlight those born in Yorkshire or works I have had the pleasure of owning. This artist's work, although a favourite, is beyond my means!

Henry Spencer Moore
1898 – 1986

Henry Spencer Moore was a pioneer with an original vision for modern sculpture, inspired by the human body and natural forms that can clearly be seen within his monumental bronze sculptures.

Born in Castleford, a small Yorkshire mining town, in 1898, he was the seventh child of eight. He knew he wanted to be a sculptor from an early age but trained as a teacher until enrolling first at the Leeds School of Art, where after a two-year drawing course he became the only full-time student studying sculpture. Winning a scholarship, he went on to study at The Royal College of Art in London.

His reputation as a sculptor grew and by the 1930s, he was one of the leading sculptors in Europe. During the Second World War, Moore became an official war artist concentrating his work on people sheltering in the London Underground stations during the blitz. His drawings captured the imagination of the public.

In the 1940s and 1950s, Moore's reputation grew as a series of public works were sited in schools, hospitals and housing estates. In 1948 he won the international prize for sculpture and the Venice Biennale.

Moore's reputation was at its peak in the 1960s as the demand for his work grew. In 1977, aged 79, Moore's success was such he decided to establish the Henry Moore Foundation, consolidating his desire to encourage the opportunities for artists and for sculpture.

Moore died in 1986.

Acknowledgements

It is always a wonderful feeling when a book is finally finished and particularly book number 13! I was, however, reassured throughout the writing process that number thirteen should hold no worries for me as it is my wife's lucky number and so any superstitions were put on the back burner.

I say this at the conclusion of every book but it cannot be emphasised enough. To finish you need to start and for that to happen an idea must be germinated. The idea for *Trapped Secrets* started after a wonderful stay at Goldsborough Hall, near Knaresborough. It was seeing a murder mystery night was planned made me wonder just how DCI Cyril Bennett would cope being encouraged to attend by Julie. I must thank Clare and Mark Oglesby who kindly allowed me to set the opening and closing scenes within their beautiful hotel and home. It will be an honour to see a copy of the book in your magnificent library.

A thank you to Donna Wilbor for being on hand to help with some of the finer details of the buses and the routes into Ripon. To John Ridley for his help with the scenes set near Fountains Abbey.

Having ideas and ensuring they are plausible is key and I must thank Pamela Clare who is famous for her media makeup skills used in both TV and films. Being able to watch her at work as well as touch hands and skin made from silicone was a fascinating experience.

Thank you to Carrie and Tony of The Harrogate Tea Rooms for their wonderful support. It's always a pleasure when Cyril pops in.

I would like to thank my advanced readers for their keen eyes, honest critique, support and kindness. In no particular order: Dee Groocock, Sarah Hardy, Lynda Checkley, Craig Gillan, Ian Cleverdon, Donna Wilbor, Caroline Vincent (my guardian angel), Susan Hunter, Susan Hampson, Susan Burns, Donna Morfett, Emma Truelove and Jennifer Sutherland.

A huge thanks must go to Debbie for carrying out the first proofread and to Helen Gray for her diligent proofing and editing – I'm so pleased she continues to say yes when asked to take on the task.

The covers of the whole series are the work of two people, firstly the man who created the smoke images, Kevin Graham and the man who designs the cover, Craig Benyon of Create Print, Wigan. Thank you both very much.

A massive thanks to book clubs, reading groups and bloggers for the work you all do on a daily basis to support the writing community. I am so very grateful for the support you continue to give to my books and your ability to bring them to a broader audience.

Thanks to Andrew Forsyth and Geoff Blakesley for your continued support.

I could go on and I would still miss some people, those hidden cogs in the wheels that make this writing machine work. To those I have missed – thank you!

Finally, it is to you dear reader that I send my sincere thanks for buying and reading my work. I try to ensure each episode can be enjoyed as a standalone read but it gives me a great deal of pleasure to hear that readers love following the lives of the main characters, characters who have become members of our family. The many kind comments I receive encourage me to write more.

If you have enjoyed this book then please tell your friends and family as word of mouth is the best way to bring more readers to my books.

Until book 14.

My best wishes,
Malcolm.

www.malcolmhollingdrakeauthor.co.uk

Printed in Great Britain
by Amazon